And The Lincoln County War

CLOWN WILLIAM

And The Lincoln County War

Robin Elno

IE Snaps

by
IngramElliott

Published by IngramElliott, Inc.
www.ingramelliott.com
9815 J Sam Furr Road, Suite 271, Huntersville NC 28078

This is a work of fiction. The names, characters, places, or events used in this book are the product of the author's imagination or used fictitiously. Any resemblance to actual people (alive or deceased), events, or locales is completely coincidental.

Book design by Maureen Cutajar, gopublished.com
Cover design by Jeanine Henning

ISBN Paperback: 978-0-9990573-3-9
ISBN E-book: 978-0-9990573-4-6

Library of Congress Control Number: 2018934546
Subjects: Fiction - Western.

Published in the United States of America
Printed in the United States of America
First Edition: 2018, First International Edition: 2018

The Clown William series by Robin Elno

Clown William
Clown William and the Lincoln County War

Coming Soon

William's adventures continue.
Look for the third book in the *Clown William* series
in 2019.

Draw Two

"Well, well, look who it is."

The words startled William awake, and he opened his eyes to find a shotgun pointed at his nose. The man with his finger on the trigger was the outlaw Jesse Evans.

William glanced quickly around the inside of the stagecoach. His precious Emily Tunstall sat rigid beside him; the two male passengers they had picked up in Santa Fe that morning shivered, ashen-faced, on the opposite bench. Their breath fogged in the New Mexico winter air.

"The other three of you ease on out the other door," Jesse said. "William, you stay put until I say."

William raised his hands, fingers splayed. He turned his head slightly so he could watch the passengers disembark.

Smiling, a scar-cheeked man wrapped in an oilskin duster waved them out with a revolver.

"Okay, William, slide out this side, real slow. Remember, I seen you draw and I know you're fast, but it just takes a twitch of my finger to blow your head off. I'm bettin' even you ain't that fast."

With exaggerated slowness, William stepped from the coach. He knew Jesse from a run-in with the outlaw in Wichita three years earlier. It had been Jesse who first strapped a gun to William's leg. And watched William kill his first man.

"Been busy since we last met," Jesse said. "And you're still wearin' Walt's gun that I gave ya."

William glanced at the driver's box. A third outlaw, coat collar turned up against the wind, held an unwavering gun pointed at the driver and man riding shotgun, both of whom had their arms stretched as far skyward as they could.

William returned his attention to Jesse, who was wrapped in a sheepskin coat topped by his silver-banded black hat. "If you had not given me a gun, Jesse, there would be fewer dead men. I probably would never have become a g-g-gunfighter."

"Hey, who knew? I thought you a pathetic clown with your twitches and hooting. I just helped you find your secret talent. Saved your life in the bargain."

"What difference does that make if you are going to kill me now?" William concentrated on staying rigid, fearful that a twitch would prod Jesse into firing the shotgun. And if there was one thing he did a lot of, it was twitch.

His vision blurred at the edges. That peculiar mental state, where his mind retreated while his reflexes exploded into a maelstrom of deadly accuracy—what William thought of as his dark tornado—neared.

Jesse smiled and took a step back, pointed the shotgun to the side, and eased the twin hammers down. "How come you ain't up top ridin' shotgun? Seems more in your line of work."

Cautious relief flooded William. He smiled but kept his hands up, hoping Jesse would continue to de-escalate the situation. "If I had been, I do not think you would have gotten the drop on us."

"That's the spirit." Jesse laughed. "Look, some cattle boss down south is looking to hire on men who have special skills with a gun. You're about as good as any. You wanna join up?"

William had just left Trinidad, Colorado, three days before—glad to escape a similar engagement working for the Atchison, Topeka and Santa Fe Railroad—and had no interest in getting back into a gunfighter harness again.

He thought of Emily and, for the first time since his rude awakening, felt a flash of fear for her safety. And guilt. He had accompanied her from Trinidad as her protector, but now that she actually needed protection, what should he do? Would revealing his connection to Emily make her a pawn—and could the information be used to force him into joining Jesse's gang? Or was being silent, leaving her to the mercy of this outlaw band, the more dangerous course?

He would deal with future threats against Emily when they happened. Her immediate safety came first. He lowered his hands to his side.

"I am already working," William said. "The lady is with me. She hired me to take her to her family." He met Jesse's eyes. "Let us continue unmolested. If you harm her, I will kill you."

Jesse's brows angled together in doubt. He glanced down at the shotgun.

Though his hands hung at his side, William gave a slight shake of his head. "That sheepskin coat will slow you down." His stare bored into Jesse. "I am that fast, and you know it."

Jesse didn't budge. "You're forgetting the passengers. You might get me, but my men will kill them all, the lady first."

"You know I cannot control my tics. My gunplay is just like them. If you push me, the choice is out of my hands. Threatening the passengers has me close to the edge." His lips twisted in an involuntary exclamation. "Yahhh." He gathered up his last vestige of control. "I do not want to shoot you, but in another few seconds, I will not be able to stop myself."

The first winds of the dark tornado swept over him. William struggled against it; Emily would die if there were any shooting. A lingering rational thought told him to stand down, surrender his gun.

Jesse turned away. "I believe you. There *is* something out of control about you. Too bad. I would love to have you on my side." He called to his man on the other side of the stage. "Bring the lady over here, gently."

William exhaled his own pent-up maelstrom as the tornado retreated, not all the way beyond the horizon, but far enough that William could think again.

Emily came around the rear of the coach, hands in the air and trailed by the scar-faced man who held her at gunpoint. She shivered from cold and fright.

Jesse said to William, "You can have her. Just stand aside and no one gets hurt. Try anything, and she dies." To the man holding the driver and rider captive, he called, "Have them start tossing down that baggage up top. Get the other two male passengers to help." He cradled the shotgun in the crook of his arm and winked at William.

The tornado was gone and William thought clearly again. He walked to Emily and stepped between her and her captor, ushering her to the side of the trail. Hands resting on his belt, he glared at the robbers. He could probably kill them all, but even if the odds were a thousand to one against Emily getting hurt in the exchange, he refused to take the chance.

William watched the outlaws rifle through Emily's luggage, strew dresses on the snow-covered ground, paw through her hat boxes, and spill the contents of the traveling bags. They took her purse that held the money her brother had sent and looted the male passengers of watches and banknotes.

Jesse picked up William's half-empty carpetbag. He peeked in. "Yours?" he asked.

William nodded.

Jesse laughed and tossed the bag at William's feet. "Not doing very well, are ya? Well, when you're done workin' for the lady, come find me. You'll get more than a sack of clothes and a few bullets. You'll get paid in gold."

The band mounted and rode off.

As soon as they were gone, William helped Emily back into the coach and out of the cold wind.

One of the male passengers, Andrew, slid in beside her. A businessman on his way to Mesilla, he wore a suited vest from which dangled an empty watch chain. He offered his outer coat to Emily.

Paul, a drover traveling south on the stage, helped the driver and shotgun man repack some of the strewn belongings and reload the top.

"What happened?" William asked the stage driver as they put Emily's dresses back into the portmanteau.

"The man with the scar was standing by the side of the road, saddle at his feet. The Barlow and Sanderson Stage Company always stops for stranded folk, and he looked to be a cowboy down on his luck. The man pulled a hidden gun when Frank, riding shotgun, reached down to help load the saddle. Next thing we knew there was three of 'em, one with a shotgun heading toward the passengers. Nothing we could do but cooperate."

William closed the lid on the portmanteau. "I guess that is why I did not get any warning there was a holdup until it was too late for me to do anything." He and the driver muscled the heavy trunk into the grasp of the two men on top of the stage; the men then secured the trunk to the baggage rails.

The driver nodded. "Least ways no one got kilt."

William settled back into the coach beside Emily. A whip cracked and the stagecoach lurched forward.

For long minutes the only sounds were the moan of the biting wind and the rumble-squeak of the iron-shod wheels as they bumped through frozen ruts on the snow-packed road.

The occupants did not speak and avoided eye contact as each sought to emerge from the shadow of the gun.

William slid his hand to encompass Emily's and squeezed gently.

Emily sighed and used her free hand to pat William's encircling fingers. When she looked at him, her pupils danced like a compass needle. From experience, William knew this meant she was searching through her mental library of classical works.

"William, I was so frightened. Those rough men had us all at their mercy. You proved yourself the valiant knight I thought when first we met. 'Women may fall when there's no strength in men.'"

William smiled. "Which Greek poet said that?"

"Not a Greek. Shakespeare. From *Romeo and Juliet*."

"I should have known. You quote him most often."

"That is because, of all the writers, he is the one most articulate of the human condition."

William looked at the other two passengers. Their dour expressions had softened, and they smiled at Emily.

"Shakespeare b-b-brightens up a stagecoach."

Emily squeezed William's hand harder. "I believe you find yourself in a perilous condition now. Who was that man you called Jesse, and what is your history with him? He is a bad man, William."

"His name is Jesse Evans, and he is the leader of a gang of outlaws. One of his men picked a gunfight with me before I carried a gun. Jesse could have stopped him, I am sure, but instead he gave me a gun and let his man try to shoot me. Eeow." William stared out the window at the bleak tundra. "God gives people gifts. He gave me both my illness and a fast draw. But did he give me my fast hand to balance my physical ailment, or my physical ailment as the price of my fast draw?"

"There remains some star-crossed fate between you and Mr. Evans." Emily's pupils began their circular dance again. "'These violent delights have violent ends and in their triumph die, like fire and powder, which as they kiss, consume.'"

"*Romeo and Juliet* again?"

Emily nodded.

"How does that story end?"

"In a pleasant catharsis for the audience." Emily sighed. "Not so well for the characters."

Minnie

Pulling into Lincoln, New Mexico, William saw a flat brown town in hilly green country. A single street, the dirt packed hard as an earthenware plate, ran between log buildings. Sheet-like storefronts, ripped from sawn boards and splashed with varnish, displayed crookedly hung signs—hand-lettered in slashes of mismatched paint. A town ugly with cold, sharp edges.

Even so, William was glad to have reached the end of the journey. He and Emily arrived on the third of February, 1878, having been bounced around in the stagecoach for more than a week, and they were bruised and stiff. The air in the compartment smelled of Emily's rosewater perfume and his masculine stink. Dust creases veined their clothes.

The stagecoach stopped directly in front of the first structure, the only two-story building William saw. A balcony, reached by stairs on either end, ran the length of the edifice and shaded the front porch. A plaque centered over the balcony read "J. J. Dolan & Co." Signs posted on the clapboards by the entrance to the lower floor proclaimed the building a store, billiard parlor, bank, and Masonic hall.

In spite of its stated multipurpose use, the building squatted, dark and foreboding. A man, maggot-white from too little sun, in shirtsleeves and pants held up by suspenders, darted from the building to collect the mail sack.

William grasped Emily's arm to steady her as she stepped down from the coach. Several people drifted over to talk to the stage driver, even though the robbery had been reported at their first overnight stop days before and the telegraph had made it old news. One man peered into the interior of the coach behind her.

Andrew and Paul got out to stretch their legs. Paul studied the signs at the entrance and went into the building.

Emily craned her neck and squinted down the length of the street. "You would think they might have taken us to the center of town," she said. "Why deposit us on the outskirts like this?"

William pointed toward the two-story building and the small crowd of people who gathered around the coach. "This is the heart of the t-t-town. Everything is downstream from here."

"Let's find John's store," Emily said. "That's the town's heart to me."

Several of the men helped unload Emily's luggage from the top of the stage, and two offered to carry it to the hotel.

"I shall be staying with my brother at the Tunstall store," she said. "Please take them there for me."

The two men glanced quickly at one another, hesitating. A third man stepped in front of them and picked up the portmanteau.

"Glad to help, ma'am," he said, his tight-lipped smile challenging the other two.

"But she's a Tunstall," one said.

"She's a lady. Now pitch in."

"Brady won't like it," said one, but they reached for Emily's luggage.

William already had two carpetbags in each hand and left one, along with three hat boxes, for the other two men. The low February sun played tricks with the gap in the surrounding hills, casting the Dolan side of the street in shade and illuminating William and Emily's destination in harsh light. They followed the three men down the center of the road where light and shadow met. The air, cold and dry, carried only meager odors.

A sign labeled the first building on their left "Lincoln Hotel, Samuel Wortley, Proprietor." Next, a square of foundation stones marked a house under construction; over the unfinished walls, the cleared lot sloped down to a narrow, shallow river whose course backed all the buildings on the left side of the street. They passed a stone house lurking in the shadows on their right; on their left, a large adobe-and-wood house with a veranda gleamed in the sun.

Stacked goods and horses tethered to hitching rails filled the open space between buildings.

A store stood on the lot next to the house with the veranda. The sign, black lettering neat on recently white-washed wood, read "Tunstall and McSween." An earthy smell of cured spices and inked cloth beckoned from the door.

"There, William," Emily said, "that is my brother's place."

The men carrying Emily's luggage dropped their burden on the wooden boardwalk in front of the store and turned to go.

The leader tipped his hat to Emily. "Here you go, ma'am." He glanced over his shoulder at the entrance to the Dolan store. "Welcome to Lincoln." He looked at the store again as two men strolled out and glared at him. "I'd better be getting back to the House."

"The house, sir?" Emily asked.

"It's what we call Dolan's place." He settled his hat on his head, and as he brushed past Emily, he whispered, "Best stay away from it."

William watched the three men start back to where the stagecoach stood. "Wonder what that was about."

Emily shrugged and turned to enter her brother's store. The two men standing near the store stared at her.

"Hoot. Would one of those men be your brother John?"

Emily shook her head. "My brother is most likely inside his store. I imagine he spends some time on his ranch, but I expect him in town today to meet us. I hope you two like each other. He won't care for me having traveled alone with you, but when I explain things to him, he will be glad you protected me."

William thought of the past week. "If you call that protection."

"Yes, I think we should," Emily said as she stepped upon the wooden boardwalk that fronted her brother's store. "Isn't this a wonderful town? So bright, like a green spring of promise. Would you bring those things inside, please?"

A young man—William guessed he was a few years older than his own age of twenty-two—bounded out of the store before Emily could enter. Just under six feet tall, thin and trim, sandy-haired and clean-shaven, he wore a business suit of dark broadcloth.

"Minnie," he exclaimed, hugging Emily. "I am so glad you made it at last." He hugged her again and kissed her cheek.

William waited, not sure what to think. The young man had called her 'Minnie.' Had he mistaken Emily for someone else? But Emily returned the embrace with equal enthusiasm. Was this her brother John? The man was much younger than William expected, as he assumed John to be Emily's much older brother.

"John, this is William," Emily said when she finally broke the embrace. "He has been a good friend; I would not have made it here but for him."

John seemed to notice William for the first time. Emily's brother cocked his head slightly for a moment, a puzzled frown on his face. "Pleased to meet you, sirrah," he said at last. "Thank you for assisting my sister." He held out his right hand.

William put the two carpetbags in his right hand on the ground and shook the offered hand. He lurched forward. "Whip, whip."

John squinted down his nose. "I beg your pardon."

William noted a white film over John's right eye. Blind on the right side, William thought. His left eye is all the keener for that, like the look he gave me.

He handed him the remaining two carpetbags. "Hoot."

"Take my belongings inside, John," Emily said, motioning to the growing pile of bags and boxes.

"Lucius," John called to someone in the store. "Please take my sister's things to my room. Quickly now." Turning back to Emily, he said, "Come on in, dearest. You must be exhausted."

"Oh yes, ever so," Emily said. She linked arms with him, and the two glided into the darker interior of the building.

William stood, alone on the boardwalk for the moment. He took a breath, shrugged, and followed with a carpetbag in each hand.

A Warm Welcome

The Tunstall store formed an L, the short arm running past the sales counter and straight to the back, where a side door led to John Tunstall's quarters. John gave this room up to Emily and laid a bedroll on the floor just outside her door.

The longer arm of the floor made a single aisle to the left of the entrance and paralleled the street for the 150-foot length of the store. It was dark—all walls too precious with shelves to allow for windows—lit only by a few stray sunbeams creeping in through small slits at the roofline. The ceiling was high and the room cool in the heavy air.

William sat in a chair leaning against the wall at the far end of this aisle and waited, watching the customers. After days of bending all his efforts on getting Emily to this town, this store, he felt at loose ends. Gathering dust, shelved like the dry goods around him.

After a week of constant companionship, William missed Emily's presence. Foreboding niggled at his mind. Now that Emily had completed her journey, she had little need of him. He felt uncertain of what he had hoped would happen— beyond the pleasure of her company and the delight of her conversation. Could men like him plan for a future? During the week with Emily, he had let his guard down and raised his hopes up. Now pain was the price of such folly.

Hours passed before John strode toward him. Emily hurried behind.

"Ah, William, you are still here," John said. "Please do not let me keep you any longer. I fear you have missed the stage, but another comes through in a few days. You may stay at the hotel while you wait."

Emily laid her hand on John's shoulder. "You should hire him, John. I brought him all this way so he could help you."

"Eeeep." William's fingers staccatoed three beats on his shirt button.

"I already have a clerk. Lucius—you met him, Minnie. I wish I did enough business to warrant a second sales-man, but alas, I do not."

"Just hire him until the next stage, and if you do not find use for him by then, he shall be on his way," Emily said without looking at William.

"Hoot, eeep." Hands clenched and relaxed, he blew out a sharp breath.

"I do not like having him around." John narrowed his eyes at Emily. "I cannot fathom what your relationship with him has been, but I think you've had quite enough of his company."

William ground his jaw. "Perhaps you would rather I stepped outside while you finish making plans for me."

"See there, John." Emily gave her brother a tart smile. "Whatever has happened to your manners? Father taught you better. I will tell you William has been more of a gentleman over the past week than you have been today."

John frowned at William and returned to the sales counter.

Emily's words sent a warm feeling down his spine. She had stuck up for him, trying to get him a position at the store. Was it to be near him? He dared hope.

Four men entered the store and broke William's reverie. His tongue signaled brewing violence with that unique hair-raised itch. He walked through the deep shadows toward the patch of light the open door threw on the counter. As William drew closer, John confronted the men, hands on his hips, jaw thrust forward.

"We're lookin' for your friend Chisum," said the man face-to-face with John. "He's been rustling cattle."

"If he mixes his in with yours," said the man beside him, a whip of a mustache snaking along his upper lip, "we'll take his herd when we take your store."

"He is simply balancing the books," John said. "He reported to me that my brand was mixed in with your herd as well."

"Papers've been filed," said the first. "Your brand won't mean anything much longer."

"You have no cause to file papers on me, Brady."

William watched the two men skulking behind Brady and his mustachioed partner. One, a rangy mutt, snuck a furtive look over his shoulder. The other slithered his gun out of its holster.

William's gun flashed from his own. "Hoot."

The four men startled and looked at him, and at his six-gun covering them. William's shoulders twitched and his Colt wavered.

The rangy mutt hitched toward his sidearm, while the one with the slithering gun sent it home to its holster. Brady shot William a murderous glare, but softly touched the arm of the man who looked ready to draw.

It surprised William to see a sheriff's star on Brady's chest.

"Everybody stay calm," Brady said, his even voice contrasting with the rage in his eyes. "What business is this of yours?"

"The Tunstalls are friends of mine," William said. "I do not like someone drawing a g-g-gun when my friends are not—" He mistimed his breathing on the last word: "Hoot."

"Tunstall, is this clown really a friend of yours?" Brady asked through sneer-curled lips.

"Hoot."

"You have delivered your message," John Tunstall said. "If you would like to purchase something, I will help you at the counter. If not, leave my store."

Sheriff Brady spat on the floor and spun on his heel. The four stalked from the store.

John glared at the back of Brady's head. Had the sheriff's head been wood, smoke would be coming from his ears.

William slid his revolver back into its leather.

John cocked his head and looked at his sister. "I understand now what you meant about employing William, Minnie." He studied William, eyes drifting down to the holstered weapon at his hip. "Care to stay the night?"

"Hoot."

The Lay of the Land

John pulled out his pocket watch at 7:00 p.m. and announced, "Time to close the store. Minnie, tonight we'll celebrate your arrival with a fine dinner at Wortley's. William, you're welcome to join us."

"Thank you, John. I would like to t-t-talk some things out, make some plans."

The trio walked back toward the Dolan end of town until John turned them up the walk at the Lincoln Hotel.

"When you said the restaurant was called Wortley's," Emily said, "I couldn't help but think the name didn't promise much in the way of fine dining."

"This shall delight you," John said. "Wortley manages the hotel, and does all the cooking. He's a wonderful cook, so everyone dines here. We just call the place Wortley's."

The dining area encompassed five round tables in the small lobby, and ten more on a wide porch between the lobby and the street. Most of the tables were occupied by diners, but John spied an empty one in the corner of the lobby and led William and Emily to it. Emily sat with her back to one wall, and John sat next to her, facing the room. He placed orders for steak and potatoes with Wortley and gestured William to sit.

William sat with his back to the room, a position that made his skin crawl. His neck twisted in a series of three tics.

John glanced sidelong at Emily.

"Those movements are involuntary," she told her brother. "I got used to them after a while."

"I would think it would be dangerous for him to carry a gun," John said, grasping her hand.

"It is," Emily said, patting his hand in return. "The tale I can tell you of Trinidad . . . But later—it is not proper dinner conversation."

William lost his appetite. He had never felt this way with Emily before. Ashamed and humiliated as an object of conversation—conversation not fit for the dinner table. More than that, an intimacy of looks between Emily and John made him uncomfortable.

Emily wore the dress with the rose pattern she had worn at the telegraph office in Trinidad. There the print had been bright and vibrant; now it seemed dull and faded.

"Father did not want me to come," Emily was saying to John when William mentally picked up the conversation. "He forbade any members of the household to accompany me, as if that would stop me. My trip was nearly derailed in Trinidad, but I found William and it worked out for the best."

"I am glad you made it." Addressing William, John said, "I am grateful to you, sir. What are your plans now? Will you be leaving soon?"

"I have no plans at the m-m-moment," William said. He heard the steady tromp of footsteps behind him. He ached to turn around.

"I suppose I could use another hand at the ranch," John said.

Might be good experience, William thought, *if* he still wanted to run a way station for a stagecoach line. The idea, though, had lost some of its appeal. "How far away is your ranch?"

"Thirty miles south of town. It is not a big place, just a large cattle pen actually, for gathering the herd for sale to the army."

"Gathering the herd? Where do you r-r-raise them?"

John smiled. "Oh, the cattle wander all over. The trick, frankly, is to round them up and keep them together long enough to sell."

"Where does Chisum fit into all this?" William knew the name. "I thought he was a T-T-Texas man."

"He was. Sold his herd and moved here to start a new ranch. He is partners with most of the small ranchers around. He also has a financial interest in my store and plans to establish a bank in Trinidad."

"The sheriff called him a r-r-rustler."

"He would—Brady is Dolan's man," John said, voice flat as the bread he buttered.

"What is going on here, John?" William asked.

"I am locked in a fight for this town. The money here is in government beef contracts. This town services all the ranches in the area. Control the town, control the ranches, and control the beef. A wonderful business opportunity, actually."

Had Emily known all this and brought him here just to get him involved in a range war? It could be worse than Trinidad. But, there would be Emily, so in some ways perhaps better too. "Eeeep." But not if he worked thirty miles out of town.

"What about your store?"

"I started the store to challenge Dolan, who has a stranglehold on the commerce here. He and his partner, Murphy, are not loosening their grips easily."

"What would you want me to do at the r-r-ranch?" William asked. "I am no rustler."

"Neither am I!" John took a steadying breath. "I need people to guard my cattle from the real rustlers." John looked into William's eyes. "You have the mien of a protector."

"Mean?" William looked to Emily at the confusing word.

"Mien," she said. "M-i-e-n. Air or bearing, appearance. From shortening the word 'demeanor.'"

This sounded more like the Emily he knew. He smiled at her and then looked back at John. "How much time would I s-s-spend away from town?"

"Most all of it." John's look was steady, calculating.

"Eeeeh." The realization John was trying to keep William away from Emily allowed the sound to escape him. He tugged on his collar three times. After a calming breath, he asked, "Would you teach me to c-c-clerk at the store instead?"

John frowned, looked past William into the dining room. "That is something about which I need to consult my partner Alex."

Footsteps closing from behind made William half turn. A man stood behind his chair, looking down at them.

"Speak of the devil," John said. "William, this is Alex McSween. Alex, join us for dinner, won't you?" He waved at the fourth, and empty, chair at the table. "Alex, this is William, who rode bodyguard for Emily from Colorado, and I am apprising him on the situation here."

Alex McSween was older than John. A bushy mustache, arched from one side of his chin to the other, dominated his face. Black hair, curly as a lamb's, lay back in a receding hairline. Like John, he wore a dark broad-cloth suit. And no gun.

John said, "Alex is the man who convinced me to come to Lincoln, and he advanced me the money for the store. He used to be Dolan and Murphy's lawyer."

"Their business started with four people," Alex said. "Murphy, Riley, and Fritz, with Dolan as their clerk. Dolan got rid of Riley, and became a partner."

Wortley delivered the steaks to the table. He eyed Alex. "Be back with another in a jiffy."

William sliced open his steak. Rich red juices flowed out. He put down his knife and fork. "While I wait for you to g-g-get your meal, tell me how you ended up p-p-partnering with Mr. Tunstall."

"After the three of them hired me as their lawyer, I quickly found I didn't like the way Murphy and Dolan did business." Alex scowled. "For example, they loan money to ranchers to make improvements on their land, rustle the stock needed to support the loan, and then foreclose on the ranch at the first missed payment. It was my paper-work that made it all legal." Alex sighed, a faraway look in his eyes. "Worse, Murphy has ties to the governor, who appoints the judges, so taking it to court is useless. The military doesn't care how the beef gets to the fort. It's first-time sale on all cattle, so there's no provenance or bills of sale to be inspected. But if a rancher did complain,

Murphy and the post commander at Fort Sumner are real tight as well. I've seen the letters."

"Meanwhile, in Lincoln, Dolan had the only store in town." John picked up the saltcellar to grind a few nuggets onto Emily's steak. "He fixed prices however he wanted. He hired the sheriff and deputies, so there is no help from the local law. A dodgy mess all 'round. Now the word is Murphy has the cancer and Dolan is running things. He changed the name of the company from 'L. G. Murphy and Company' to 'J. J. Dolan and Company' just last September."

Alex cut in. "And that's when I left. I knew I could never work for Dolan. With Murphy, you were safe as long as you were on the inside. But Dolan gobbles up partners near as fast as ranchers."

Alex's steak arrived.

William cut his into small pieces. "What about the third p-p-partner, Fritz? Where is he now?" He forked a small bite of steak to his mouth, nearly stabbing himself in the process.

Alex chuckled, but then stopped and sucked in an embarrassed breath. He winced, glanced at John.

John nodded in sympathy, a short eye roll saying "What can ya do?"

Alex looked back at William, face set. "Emil Fritz died in '74. Left a life-insurance policy, and Murphy sent me to

31

New York to collect on it. I did, and as instructed by Dolan, the money was transferred to my account. The court did not order me to give it to anyone, but I tried to give it to Fritz's brother. He refused it. He told me Dolan had already sent him the payment. When I came back to Lincoln, Dolan denied any contact with Fritz's brother and accused me of embezzling the funds."

William carefully laid down his fork and scratched the back of his neck. "Things in town sound pretty lopsided. John offered me a job on his r-r-ranch, but I think I would be more help if I stayed around here. I could clerk at the store."

"Doing what?" Alex said. "Don't need a sales clerk. We have Lucius. And I do the books myself."

"I was telling William his talents lie more in the protection end," John said. "There won't be any violence in town. I need his hand on the ranch."

"Brady's deputy was going to d-d-draw on you in the store today, John."

John looked at Emily in alarm. "Nonsense," he said before she could react. "Dolan and his crowd are a bunch of wankers, certainly, but as long as they have the law fixed on their side, why would they resort to murder and lawlessness?" He laid a reassuring hand on Emily's arm. "Legal paper still counts here, but out on the range, it's the law of the six-gun." He turned to William. "I hear that you are a fair lawyer in that court."

William turned to Emily, who blushed redder than the print of her dress. "It is not the c-c-career I choose."

"Sometimes the job chooses the man, William," John said.

Two New Friends

"You need a horse," John said to William when he entered the store the next morning.

William's shoulder pulled tight in a tic, and his face scrunched. "Not much of a rider."

"Can you handle a horse?" John asked. "This valley is twenty miles long, and you shall need to cover every foot of it."

"I can manage if the mount is well b-b-broken."

"I am certain we can find you something." John led William out the back door of the store to a small corral with a hay rack, water tub, and several horses.

Emily followed. "Are these all yours? They're so scruffy."

John gave the stock a quick glance. "Sometimes the customers leave their horses here while they take care of business, but yes, these are all mine."

"You keep the good ones on the ranch, then." Emily's lips pouted. "But why not ride your best to town?"

"These horses are just paints. Not the most reliable of horses. I use them for loaners, or quick sales. Somebody comes by stage and needs to travel to an outlying ranch, I rent him a paint. Or loan one to a customer who needs an extra horse to get their purchases home. I also sell them with a promise to buy them back at half price if returned."

Emily nodded. "So you keep your Arabians on the ranch, then."

The smile that John gave Emily reminded William of his own mother sneaking him a sweet biscuit behind his father's back. Conspiratorial and indulgent.

"I was waiting for you to arrive before I started breeding Arabians," John said to his sister.

A look William did not understand passed between Emily and her brother.

William, uncomfortable as an unwanted guest, turned his attention to the horses.

A brown-and-white mare with black points nipped at a small stallion, a leopard Appaloosa, which had attempted to crowd her from the hayrick. A brown horse, with white forelock and a spilled inkblot of black covering his back, raised its head to look at William, lips pulled back to catch his scent. The horse's teeth splayed forward.

Too young, too restive, too old, William thought as he looked them over. A tic caused him to stumble, and he clutched at the top rail of the corral for balance. The young stallion gave a hard, sharp chuff of alarm, and all the horses shuffled nervously, except one.

A black-pointed gelding, light brown markings looking like butterflies chasing over a field of white on its back and withers, chewed slowly while regarding William steadily with one brown and one green eye.

William wished he had some morsel to offer the horse to cajole it over for a closer look. His jaw spasmed. "Castrated carrot," he said. "Hoot."

John laughed beside him. "You would name a horse Castrated Carrot?"

William grinned, embarrassment coloring his neck. "I was wishing for something to feed him, so I could have a b-b-better look," he said, pointing to the gelding.

John pulled a lump of sugar from his pocket and handed it to William. "Be my guest. That one is named Sunfish."

As William enticed the gelding over with the sugar, Emily asked, "Why do you call him Sunfish? The horse isn't big and round, or even yellow."

"We did not christen him Sunfish for his looks," John said. "Rather, it bespeaks a rebellious past. He didn't take well to the bridle. We call it a sunfish when a horse attempts to dislodge a rider by rolling on its back so it exposes the belly to the sun. But this horse is well broken now."

Sunfish ambled over to William. The horse toyed at the sugar lump with his large upper lip for a moment, then scooped it up with his lower. William glimpsed the front teeth, which met at a thirty-degree angle. About seven years old, William judged. Fifteen hands tall.

Three spasms contorted William's face, leaving him feeling like a sneeze was coming on. As he fought back the urge, he saw Sunfish turn his head to look into William's eyes. Yes, William thought, gently stroking the forehead, one sunfish to another.

"Are you really going to name him Castrated Carrot?" Emily asked.

"Sunfish is fine," William said, though disappointment in Emily roiled within him. What had happened to her? She had learned to tell his unintentional vocalizations and his purposeful speech apart. Had their mutual under-standing—so carefully nurtured over the last several weeks—been so quickly lost?

"I shall throw in the saddle and tack as part of your wages," John said. "You shall need more than one horse, but Sunfish is a sufficient start. When can you leave for the ranch?"

William grunted in disappointed acceptance. "Soon as someone shows me the way, I guess. Who is in charge there when you are g-g-gone?"

"Dick Brewer's my foreman. I have new dry-goods stock coming in today, but I shall take you out to the ranch tomorrow, introduce you around." A puff of wind tousled John's hair.

"I had better get used to r-r-riding Sunfish, then." William smiled, sighing inside. And used to being alone, he thought.

*   *   *

William, saddling up Sunfish for his first ride, recalled a mount took its commands by the movements of the rider. Because of his tics, he seldom rode. He hoped he didn't confuse Sunfish. They had only one afternoon to reach an understanding.

When William climbed on, the wide spread of his hips and legs reminded him that sitting a horse was more intense than sitting in a chair. The feeling of bulk, of power between his thighs, made him surge with the excitement that gave his tongue that familiar hair-on-end tingle. But this time he had no urge to grab for his gun.

He gathered the reins in his hands. Just that slight lift of the bit brought the horse's head up. William moved the reins toward the right, shifted his weight in the same direction, and pressed his left leg against Sunfish's side.

The horse responded immediately, stepping with its front feet toward the right and pivoting on its hindquarters.

If he could walk, he could ride, William thought. After all, his twitches didn't make him fall, most of the time.

A sudden tic drove William's right knee toward the horse's shoulder. Sunfish jerked his head up and stopped. William waited a moment, and then repeated the pressure with his left leg and reins. Sunfish once again began to turn.

An involuntary twitch of his arm pulled the left rein tight, and Sunfish's head rose, stopping the horse dead in his tracks.

William slackened the reins, and Sunfish lowered his head again. William lightly pressed his right leg against the horse, and Sunfish returned to a slow pivot. This is not going too badly, William thought, leaning back in the saddle. Sunfish instantly stopped. William leaned forward and patted his horse's neck. "Good boy." Sunfish started walking. William leaned back and the horse stopped.

The secret was in the legs, not the reins. With very little tension on the reins, he used leg pressure by shifting his weight to turn the horse toward the corral gate.

A twitch of William's shoulder gave momentary unequal tension on the reins. Sunfish stopped and turned his head, touching his nose to William's boot. Then the horse continued out of the corral.

William rode Sunfish at a walk, trot, and lope. He relaxed in the saddle as much as his long habit of deliberate movement would allow. He gave direction to his horse. Sunfish handled the details.

William returned to the corral behind Tunstall's store around five o'clock. After brushing Sunfish down and loading fresh hay into the rick, he patted the horse a fond farewell. Then he walked the short distance to the back door and entered the store.

Emily attended to a lady in the front of the shop, while Lucius pulled a sample of wire from a shelf to show to a rancher. Several wooden crates sat with their tops pried off, cotton-fiber packing strewn about, as John sorted through the contents.

"You have returned, I see," John said, looking up from his kneeling position. "How was the ride?"

"It went well. Thank you for the horse. Anything I c-c-can do to help with the unpacking?"

"Certainly. Just pull the items out of the crates and stack them on the floor. When Lucius gets a moment, he'll show you where to put them on the shelves." John rose and put his hands on the small of his back, stretching. "When we finish here, we shall take our evening meal. I have something for you, afterwards."

They locked up the store at seven again and walked to Wortley's. This time they found a table on the covered porch. William sat facing the street, his back to the wall that separated the porch from the lobby.

Lincoln's only street ran east to west, the town closed in so tightly by low hills that there were places where the valley was only five hundred paces across. The narrow gap in the hills funneled the setting sun's light into a golden glow that lingered after the hills were dark.

The light brought little warmth as the winter wind rolled through the street. Waist-high wood-burning heaters dotted the porch, sending out small circles of cheer. Little of it reached William.

"It's a cold wind—and lonely," John said. "When it blows, you need your friends around you."

William smiled, looking at John and Emily. Friends. Did he dare allow friendship with the Tunstalls to grow? The sheriff in Trinidad had reminded William his kind didn't have friends. He thought of Washburn, the reporter killed when mistaken for William. A dangerous thing, friendship. And as recent experience with Emily proved, the risk of being hurt cut both ways.

Maybe better to stick with a gunfighter's usual friends—a horse and a gun.

After dinner, John led them back to the store. He pulled a wooden box from beneath the counter. "I just received these, and I have not yet put them on display. I ordered several different brands from Santa Fe. You shall have first pick."

John laid several new revolvers, still in packing grease,

on the counter. Most looked flatter, the butts less gracefully curved, than the Colt William carried.

"These are the newest thing—double-action revolvers," John said. "Pulling the trigger both cocks the hammer and fires the gun. When you work for me, I want you armed with the dandiest gear. What is your opinion of them?"

Cold and heartless, he thought, and not just because the flatter butt emphasized the mechanical nature of the hammer and cylinder assembly. No doubt it made the gun more efficient, but robbed it of a familiar beauty. The offer of the gun reminded him of the nature of his efficient but heartless relationship to John Tunstall.

William forced a smile and considered the new weapons. How much faster would a double action make a gunman? Did it eat into the advantage he had with the single-action pieces? Were these new revolvers three times uglier?

Two of the new revolvers that retained his Colt's graceful lines caught his eye. He picked up the first one. The same size and weight as his Peacemaker, and if held side by side, they looked nearly identical.

"I might give this one a try," he told John, who handed him a rag to clean off the grease.

"That is a Colt Bisley," John said. "It's a .44 caliber."

William fumbled it back to the counter. "My Colt is a .45—too much trouble to carry two d-d-different size bullets."

He picked up the second pistol that piqued his interest. "Is this a .45?"

John nodded. "A new Remington model. Jolly good. Have a go at the ranch tomorrow; see what you think." He pulled a belt and holster from a shelf. "This should fit."

Home on the Range

The next morning, Wednesday, February 5, William rode with John to his ranch through country where, though rolling hills changed the scenery every mile, the effect remained the same. The Tunstall ranch lay south of town on the banks of the Rio Feliz. Happy River, William thought, must have been named before the ranchers moved in.

The land was well watered, and green. A ranch house of adobe and dark oak overlooked a dry dust corral surrounded by a skeletal fence of bleached wood.

The barnlike bunkhouse was long, narrow, and built of clapboard. Several men working in and around the corral stopped their chores when the party rode up. All the men wore guns.

A large, sunburned cowboy greeted them first. "Mr. Tunstall, did your sister arrive safely?" He looked up at the riders, shading his eyes with his hand, even though he wore a brimmed hat.

"That she did, Dick," John's voice boomed. He indicated William with a wave of his hand. "She brought this fellow with her. I've hired him on as another guard."

First impressions, William thought. He might be working with these men for some time.

He pushed the tip of his tongue against his teeth, willing it to be still. A neck and torso twitch betrayed him.

"Really?" Dick asked.

William gave him a grim smile. "Surprised me too."

When John made the round of introductions, William remembered two in particular. The sunburned foreman, Dick Brewer, eyed him with a suspicious curiosity. And Billy McCarty, a thin young boy with teeth like a squirrel and nutty eyes, greeted him with a jovial smile.

Billy led William to the bunkhouse. Beds lined the two long walls, bedrolls and pillows marking out territory. Between each set of bunk beds, heavy trunks of scarred wood stood guard. At each end of the room a coffeepot sat atop an iron stove. White plaster sealed the bare clapboard walls. A few windows let in slanting sunlight. The room smelled of leather with faint undertones of sweat.

"Bathhouse through there." Billy pointed to a wooden door at the far end of the bunkhouse. He showed William an empty bunk and eyed his belongings as William unpacked. Billy pointed to the new revolver in its stiff, unweathered holster. "Hey, Mr. Tunstall told me he was gonna order a few of these. You try it yet?"

"Just g-g-got it yesterday," William said.

"You nervous or something?" Billy asked, taking a step back. "Don't worry, I don't bite."

William smiled, pointing to the gun Billy carried. It was small, like him. "You ever use that thing?"

Billy shrugged. "Once or twice."

Another gunman? William wondered. A bit young for that. "What exactly do you do around here?"

"Don't worry; I do a man's work. I think you're gonna like working for Mr. Tunstall."

"Maybe. Never really worked *for* anyone before."

"Been a drifter myself." Billy sat on one of the bunk beds. "But it's nice to belong, you know? Think this time I'll do what my ma told me. Live like a postage stamp."

"Hoot. What do you mean?"

"Stick with one thing until you get there." Billy stood. "How come ya hoot?"

"God's way of telling me how much he loves me. Does it bother you?"

"Nope. I admire a cursed man." Billy took his gun from

47

his holster and twirled it around his finger. "Ya wanna have a shootin' contest?"

William considered. So Billy *was* another gunman. How many did Tunstall have working for him? But this boy seemed to think of it as a game.

"I do not shoot for sport." William picked up his new revolver from the bunk. "But I would l-l-like to try this out."

"C'mon, then, there's a place out back."

William strapped the new holster to his left thigh, looping the belt over the worn leather that held his old Colt on his right.

A cottonwood tree in back of the bunkhouse sported several oval-shaped wooden targets nailed to it. William took a deep breath, then drew his Colt as fast as he could. Five hits on five targets in a second and a half.

A low whistle from Billy. "That's some fine shootin'."

William then switched revolvers and tried fast drawing the Remington. The double action felt awkward. His first shot hit the target, but the second went wild. His habit of knocking back the hammer with his thumb in the split second before pulling the trigger spoiled his aim.

He steadied himself and tried again. The double action made setting the hammer in place for subsequent shots unnecessary. He had to consciously keep his thumb out of the play; when he did, he kept his aim true. He couldn't tell if the double action helped or hindered his speed after the first shot. He wondered if it was wise to carry two such dissimilar weapons.

For now, he would keep the Colt as his primary and carry the Remington for backup. He figured by the time he needed that second, speed would no longer be an issue. His familiar Colt slung on his right side; he strapped the new Remington on his left.

Billy's gun was a short, snub-nosed revolver, a .41 caliber made by Colt and sold under the name "The Thunderer." Its small size fit Billy's hand well, and the kid could sling it around to target with marvelous speed. The short barrel made it unreliable at any distance over ten feet, but William had no doubt that at close range Billy was deadly.

"Mind if I try that new double action?" Billy asked.

William handed the Remington over.

After a few shots, Billy handed it back. "I think I'll stay with the one that brought me," Billy said. "We dance well together."

Fortress

The feeling of ever-present danger William had felt in town was not present on the Tunstall ranch. Fitting in with a group of working men was a new experience. In the past, he was usually alone, but if not, then it had been like Trinidad—employed by one side or another, but never actually included in a group.

Dick Brewer, the foreman, treated him well, just pausing for a moment if one of William's tics distracted him.

The two Coe brothers laughed and winked at each other, sometimes miming William's twitches and trembles.

Billy, though, was another story. After target practice on the first day, he took William to meet the cook.

"Sam, this is William. Don't know his last name."

When the cook extended his hand to shake William's, Billy bumped William hard enough to cause him to stumble and miss Sam's hand.

"Hoot," William said, regaining his balance.

Billy laughed. "William Hoots. Or maybe just Hoots for short."

William drew back, an angry flush rising in his face. But the smile on Billy's face, the playful wink of an eye, flushed the anger away. A joke. Certainly not the first ever played on him, but the first done without malice—an offer of companionship more significant than a handshake.

"Only my friends call me Hoots," William said. "More than once, that is."

Sam looked at his unshaken outstretched hand in confusion.

William shook Sam's hand. "Call me Hoots."

Sam smiled and shook William's hand vigorously.

At supper that night, William's steak covered his plate.

Billy clapped William on the shoulder. "Well, Hoots, looks like you made another friend."

"I cannot eat all this," William said and sliced off a third of his portion and slid it onto Billy's plate.

That night in the bunkhouse, when William laid his head down, his pillow was hard and lumpy. He reached inside the case and pulled out a dead barn owl.

"What's the matter, Hoots?" Billy called from the next bunk over. "Birds of a feather and all."

Good-natured chuckling circulated around the bunkhouse. "It's a lot better than being wet-sheeted, like they did to me on my first night," the younger Coe brother called.

"And I don't want to tell ya what I found in my boots the morning after," laughed his older brother.

"Ya see, we was kind of hopin' you'd let us all call you Hoots," Billy said.

"We will see." William tried to sound gruff. But his voice cracked with pleasure.

Friends? Real friends? A tension he had grown accustomed to over the past three years eased away.

Relaxed, William slept deeply.

Friday dawned in rosy pink. Dick Brewer told the ranch hands that the corral needed to be strengthened in preparation for the cattle roundup the following week.

Posts needed setting, rails split. Nervously, William eyed the heavy axe and mauls. He shot a questioning look at foreman Brewer and smiled wryly.

Brewer shrugged. "Everybody pulls his own weight here."

"I have no objection to swinging the maul," William said. "But I have never found anyone willing to hold the wedge."

"I'll hold it," Billy said. "I'll be safe as kittens. You've got the truest aim of anyone I've ever seen. If you can't hit the spike dead center every time, I'll buy everybody a round of drinks in town tomorrow."

William frowned and picked up the heavy sledge. Billy did not know what he was risking. William had never been able to make anyone understand what he called his dark tornado, and knew from experience that it only appeared when his own life was on the line.

Billy positioned the spike. He smiled with confidence.

In William's mind's eye, he saw the sledge swing, smashing Billy's hands, pulping his knuckles. William froze, staring at the small target the wedge head presented. His jaw tensed, his eyes crossed. Sweat broke out on his brow.

His arms were leaden with indecision. Everyone stared at him.

"C'mon, Hoots, do it," the younger Coe brother said.

William looked away, focusing on the horizon. His heart pounded, his ears buzzed. He feared he would melt from the tension. He had never felt so helpless since his first gunfight, before he knew about his special talent. He feared for Billy, whose life now mattered to him, and in this fear, the dark tornado descended.

"Do it now!" Brewer shouted.

Without thought, without further deliberation, he swung the heavy iron down. It struck the spike perfectly, seemingly at the same instant his eyes focused on the target.

"Knew ya could," Billy said. He repositioned the wedge.

William sighed in relief. Thinking too much was his enemy. He swung again, focusing on the target after the head of the sledge was already in motion. He loosened up, swung a third time, trusting himself.

He got into a rhythm. The trick was to not think about it, but not let his mind wander either. The mental work of it exhausted him quickly. At the first quiver of fatigue, he stopped.

McCloskey spelled him on the maul, and William set to hammering the split rails to the posts. He had proven worthy of Billy's trust, and from that ember, warmth flowed outward as from a campfire. Each blow of metal on metal deepened his contentment.

That night, while William bathed, someone stole his pants. William bristled, feeling foolish, and stormed into the bunkhouse.

His pants, neatly brushed and folded, lay on the foot of his cot. He looked around, eyes stinging. "Who did this?"

Billy laughed. "Your pants were so full of critters they crawled in here on their own. We had us a real rodeo to get 'em settled down."

The elder Coe brother stood up. "Welcome to the Tunstall ranch, Hoots."

*   *   *

On Saturday morning, most of the hands, William among them, rode to Lincoln. Looking forward to seeing Emily again, he rode Sunfish straight to the corral behind the Tunstall store.

He didn't find her at the store—just Lucius who busied around a few early customers—so William pulled up a chair at the far wall and waited. He heard muffled voices from outside through the air slits at the roofline and the buzz of flies exploring the dry goods on the shelves. His mind wandered.

On his ride into town, William had noticed a squat, round tower built of sunbaked brick that sat two lots east of Tunstall's store. It looked ancient, an old fortification. It was separated from the Tunstall store by a private residence, but stood close enough that it provided a position overlooking John's front walk. He wondered if Emily's brother had begun to take such matters into consideration.

A woman's laughter broke his train of thought. It might have been Emily, but he wasn't sure. The laughter was muffled and came through the air slits from outside. Curiosity sent him to investigate.

William left the store and turned right, heading toward the west—which he now thought of as the Dolan side of town. The building adjacent to the Tunstall store was the adobe-and-wood house surrounded by verandas. He could hear the merriment more clearly now—Emily's unbridled laughter.

Emily stood chatting with a woman whose hair was piled high in a bun. As the woman talked and smiled, her hands absently smoothed the skirts of a dark-blue traveling dress with a yellow-trimmed décolletage.

William stood, unsure of whether to call to Emily, when John's partner, Alex, came out of the house and approached the two women on the veranda. As he did so, he saw William.

"William, come on up. Like you to meet my wife."

"Hoot," William said, and started up the walk to the porch.

The woman talking to Emily swung around to watch him. Her nose was broad; a sweep of eyebrow arched above her widely separated green eyes. She smiled pleasantly.

"This is my wife, Susan," Alex said, beaming. "She's been in Santa Fe on store business. Susan, this is William, a friend of Emily who is now working for John."

"Pleased to m-m-meet you," William said, tipping his hat.

Mrs. McSween stared at his two gun belts. "Here's a man who knows what's going on," she said to her husband.

Bewildered, William looked to Alex, who sighed heavily.

"Everyone carries a gun here," Alex said to his wife.

"Except you and John."

William felt like an intruder in family business. His face twitched, and he turned to go.

Emily touched his arm, stopping him.

"Will you walk me back to the store?" she asked.

William looked at the store, barely fifteen yards away. "Of course." Then he redirected his gaze to Alex and Susan. "If you will excuse us. It was nice to meet you, Mrs. McSween."

Susan nodded an acknowledgment of the courtesy, and then with an icy stare at her husband, strode into the house. Alex smoothed his mustache and followed her.

Though curious about this interplay between Alex and his wife, William shrugged it off and offered his arm to Emily.

It took only a few moments to reach the store entrance, too little time for much talk. William, wanting Emily's company, looked around for inspiration to keep her engaged in conversation. His glance fell on the squat, crude tower nearby. "What do you know about that t-t-tower?" he asked.

"It's called the Torreon. My brother told me the earliest Hispanic settlers built it for protection from raiding Apaches.

It used to be the center of a plaza in the old days. The *jacales* are gone, and now only that old, crumbling tower remains. Too bad—the loss of the settlers' mud huts reminds me of the impermanence of things here in the West."

William smiled. This sounded more like the old Emily. "Will you join me for d-d-dinner?" he asked.

Emily frowned. "John and I are having dinner at the McSweens'."

Fearing his disappointment would show on his face, William nodded and turned away.

Again, she touched his arm. "I shall ask Susan. I think she'd like to have you there." The store swallowed her before he could ask her to explain why she thought so.

He debated following her in and perhaps helping out a bit with the dry goods. Would he be welcome? Perhaps she expected him to follow. But when she did not call to him, he walked away.

The Torreón invited exploration. When he first saw it, he thought it a huge kiln and wondered at the pottery that warranted such an oven. It was an ugly thing, a giant wasp's nest of daub and dried mud. A single door opened on the back side, and he peered in. To his right a permanent ladder—steep stairs without a rail—led to a second floor through an open trapdoor in the ceiling. Narrow slit windows spaced every forty-five degrees around the circular perimeter provided a view in all directions. There were no furnishings, and the floor was hard dirt. Broad overhead beams supported the upper floor.

William tried the steep stairs, uneasy at the lack of rails. He used his hands to haul himself up, waist high, through the trap. The upper story was like the first— firing slits spaced every forty-five degrees—enclosed by a fireproof roof of earth and dried mud. Cobwebs told of the building's lack of use in many years.

He ascended the remaining steps and peered through one of the firing slits. He could see over the whitewashed house next door and had a clear view of the front of the Tunstall store. The thick walls narrowed the view, made looking through the port like staring down a tunnel. A rifle stuck through could cover a wide arc, but the sharp-shooter who fired it would have terrible peripheral vision. A spy, however, had all the view he needed.

William returned to the first floor, wondering why no one slept in the building. It seemed to be good shelter, and apparently nobody cared about who went in or out. He paced around the lower floor, seeing there were no holes or rocks where rattlesnakes would den. There were plenty of spiders, though. Not the worst place he had ever slept.

Standing in the doorway and looking out, William saw Sunfish in the corral behind the Tunstall store. The wood frame house next door, solid on its stone foundations, blocked his view of the store itself. Remembering that he had yet to attend to Sunfish after the ride from the ranch, he left the sheltering den of the tower.

When he finished grooming his horse, William carried his saddle and tack toward the store, planning to leave it on the back veranda. As he approached, Emily appeared, framed in the back door, and waved him inside.

Sunlight pushed tentative territory into the dark interior. He faced Emily at the border, where it faded to shadow.

"Susan has added you to the guest list tonight. Dinner at seven. You have most of the day until then for your own affairs."

"I would like to help out here in the s-s-store."

Emily smiled. "That'd be fine. The store's getting quite busy, and Susan could use help at the front, packing and loading."

"Seems the least I can do for my d-d-dinner."

William worked as the outside man. He loaded wagons, tended the horses trusted to the corral, carried goods to waiting buckboards—anything that involved leaving the confines of the store. With William taking on those chores, John and Alex kept to the private office in the back room, the women avoided exposure to the street, and Lucius—selling guns and ammunition at a brisk pace—

was preserved for in-store duties. Each trip into the open air disclosed a retreating sun and lengthening shadows, and sullen-eyed men loitering across the street.

Susan left at five to prepare dinner, and John closed the store at seven. Walking the short distance to the McSweens' home, William smelled an incense of pine on the cool air.

The McSweens' adobe-and-wood house nestled in the square embrace of the veranda, where herbs hanging in clay pots swayed to the foot's tread upon the boards. The vigorous aroma of rosemary and the pitchy fragrance of basil scented the breeze.

Inside, a Saltillo-tiled floor shone like a puddle, and William's reflection slid along from one tile to another as he walked. Alex ushered them into the dining room, where the polished wood of a table as big as a double coffin gleamed in the unsteady light of lantern-hung sconces; the sconces' flames peeped over wicks turned high, as if looking for their next meal.

One picture hung on the wall, a lone steer staring at a sunset over a high mesa.

Chairs beckoned the diners, hard rail backs and seats softened by tufted cushions held on with ties at the corners. On the table, yellow roses chased around the edges of pearlescent china in an arena of silver flatware.

Bowls of beans and plates of cornbread sat within

reach. Susan brought in a platter of steaks; Alex uncorked some wine.

William had not had wine before. He sipped it politely, trying to ignore the sour taste. The rich flavor of the steaks drove any lingering unpleasantness from his palate—and beans, swimming in a sweet sauce with bacon, tucked in all the corners of his hunger.

A buttermilk pie laced with the nutty flavor of pecans followed. When Alex poured another round of wine, William let his sit.

As if the serving of the wine released her from the feminine role, Susan held up her glass to make a toast. "To the success of our enterprise, and the ruin of the Dolan gang."

William dared a large swallow to honor the toast, freezing his face in a smile in expectation of the wine's bitterness. His face quickly changed to genuine pleasure, for the wine was as agreeable as the sentiment.

"And to a safe return from Mesilla," John said, tilting his glass toward Alex.

"I don't see why you should go," Susan said to her husband. "Judge Bristol is a Dolan man. You'll get no justice from him."

"Since he signed my arrest warrant, I have no choice," Alex said, fingers white on the stem of the wine glass. "Got to clear it up or else Dolan could legally come against me."

"Arrest warrant?" William looked from Alex to John, remembering something Sheriff Brady had said. "I thought the p-p-papers filed against you were just a property dispute."

"It is complicated," John said. "The papers against me are a civil matter. The papers against Alex are another thing entire."

"Based on the criminal charges Dolan has brought against me," Alex said. "About that trumped-up embezzlement claim."

"If the charges stick, they could claim John's store profited from the money, and his goods would also be forfeited to Dolan," Susan said. "And of course, the charges'll stick because the judge does what Dolan says."

Alex swirled the remaining wine around in the bottom of his glass. "That's a decision I can appeal, so enforcement gets delayed. Because I appeared in court, the warrant for my arrest is invalidated."

"Dolan is getting the upper hand," Susan said with a hard stare at her husband.

"He has always had the upper hand. We are the newcomers, fighting against an entrenched enterprise. But if we can get this into the higher courts above those that Dolan controls, then we'll have a level cricket field," John said. He looked at Emily. "Like a gambit in chess."

Emily smiled, reached for her brother's hand, and gave it a squeeze.

"Won't you at least carry a gun until this gets settled?" Susan said, looking to both her husband and John.

"I shall not," John said. "I shall let the law do my fighting."

"Alex?" Susan's eyes were pleading, the stern set of her lips now broken by the barest quiver.

Alex sighed. "I won't carry one in town, but I'll take one along to Mesilla. In case of rattlers."

"Will you go with him?" Susan asked, turning to William.

William nearly tipped over his wine glass as disappointment flashed through him. "Hoot." So this was why Susan had invited him to supper—not for his company, but for his gun hand. And John would agree, sending William even farther from Emily.

"I won't have it," Alex said before William could respond. "Taking a gunfighter along to court won't help my case."

"I don't want you going alone," Susan said. "Once you step into that courtroom, anything could happen. Best you have a friend along."

John turned his good left eye from Alex to William. "Sorry, Susan, but I need William on the ranch this week. Need to get a herd together."

William smiled in gratitude at not being sent away.

"I'll be fine," Alex said. "I'll take Lucius as a witness. You two women can manage the store for a few days."

"You and your chess games," Susan said, standing abruptly. "These are people who don't play by the rules."

Seeing their hostess standing, the men rose to their feet.

Dinner must be over, William thought. "Thank you for the wonderful d-d-dinner, Mrs. McSween."

"Where are you staying tonight?" Susan asked.

William thought of the Torreón. "I found a place."

"Nowhere outside, I hope," Susan said. "It's February."

"He is sleeping in the store," Emily said, then turned to William. "You can play chess with John."

Thinking of building a small fire in the oven-like Torreón, William had no concerns about the cold. Though Emily meant well, no one had considered his thoughts on the matters discussed that evening. He was but a piece in a larger game. "Thank you, Emily, but I wish to be no imposition. I can manage." He paused, looking at John. "But I could use a chess lesson."

The Tunstall Ranch

On Sunday, William saw Alex and Lucius off for Mesilla. By early afternoon, the other men from John's ranch who'd weekended in town gathered at the store. Some laughed, some groaned, some showed new bruises. John, who planned to stay in town to work the store during Alex and Lucius's absence, gave instructions to his foreman, Brewer, on the week's work.

The ranch hands saddled up, and William rode back to the ranch with them.

Billy, one of the hands who finished the weekend laughing, handed several carrots to William during the ride. "Heard you wanted to castrate these."

The two nearest riders laughed, one wincing due to bruises.

Billy waved a carrot over his head and whooped. "But Molly near castrated Dirty Steve's carrot at the whorehouse last night," he said, pointing at one of the hands. Now everyone laughed, including Dirty Steve.

"Yep, they're callin' it the Clown special," Billy went on to more laughter.

William felt his cheeks blush and said, "Hoot. Guess I will stay away, then."

"Figured as much," Billy said. "So I brought the carrots for your horse, seein' as you were saving yours."

"Don't know about that," said a round-faced horse-sitter named McCloskey. "He's been hanging around the boss's sister."

William didn't understand the remark, but anger flashed through him at the tone. The message slid across his thoughts, leaving a nasty slime.

The other cowboys fell silent, but McCloskey kept at it. "How'd you get her brother outta the way?"

Using the butt of his Thunderer, Billy whacked McCloskey on the head, spilling him to the ground. "Some people don't know when to shut up."

McCloskey stood up, rubbing his head and glaring at Billy. "The next time you pull that gun on me, you'd better shoot me with it."

Billy blew him a kiss.

William rode the rest of the way in silence, turning

over what McCloskey had said. It struck a discordant note deep within him—perhaps an observation that he had previously made but buried like scat at a campsite. Something was askew between Emily and John.

The ranch hands enjoyed leisure time on Sunday night. Most gathered for a game of cards. William and Billy played chess; William's attention wasn't fully on the game, and he lost his queen early.

*   *   *

That week they pulled herd. On Monday and Tuesday, William rode with seven other hands through the wild hills and green valleys, chasing down the river courses where the strays watered. Wandering cattle in small groups—hard to think of a group of less than ten as a herd—bunched like low-hanging fruit. They drove the unresisting cattle back to the ranch, where the herd tripled over the two days.

William did not like this duty and feared his horsemanship was inadequate. Sunfish, though, knew the task and made William look good, so long as he let the reins hang very loose. Nevertheless, there were skills to being a cowboy that William did not have and which Sunfish could not supply. Neither he, nor his horse, could throw a rope on the fly.

The cattle seemed indifferent to him. They moved as directed with a nonchalance that he feared to trust. A thousand-pound steer had little respect for a man with a gun and a reputation.

On Wednesday William rode guard on the herd at the ranch while other hands brought in the last of the strays. With Sunfish quiet and steady under him, he practiced drawing while in the saddle. He did not fire for fear of spooking the cattle. And without firing, he could not test his usual proficiency.

When off duty, he asked Billy for advice. They rode a mile out from the herd, where Billy propped several stones in the low branches of a tree.

Billy had no trouble drawing and firing from horseback. He rode close to his target, made his draw smooth and deliberate, and once his gun was clear, was as accurate as standing still.

Seeing that a fast draw from horseback was impractical, William used the Remington on his left side. He pulled it from its holster by reaching across his stomach with his right hand. As he drew it back to aim, he had plenty of time to cock the hammer. After the first shot, the double action did the rest. Once his revolver was free in his hand, he could point and fire as fast as on the ground. William had never analyzed the elements of his draw before; now he realized that his speed with a gun lay in the rapidity with which he could target-point.

The first time he fired, Sunfish leapt in a single nervous

buck. But even on the convulsive leap, William's shot was true, blowing the stone from its perch in the tree at twice Billy's distance. He reloaded, also a bit tricky while in the saddle, and continued to practice. After his eighth shot, Sunfish calmed, barely twitching at the report of the gun. It must be that the motion of reaching across his belly to draw alerts the horse to what's coming, William thought. And then the tighter grip of his legs, to brace for the recoil, signaled the shot to follow.

William leaned down to stroke Sunfish's neck. Smart horse.

On Thursday a squadron of weathered cowboys rolled onto the ranch in their own dust storm. Sent by John Chisum to gather up Tunstall's cattle, they were to join them with the larger herd, and drive them to Fort Sumner to fulfill the February 15 contract for beef for the Indian reservations.

William rode guard on the periphery of the herd while the Chisum professionals sorted through Tunstall's gathered cattle, tallying how many head belonged to each of the small ranchers. Dolan's cattle, and there were many, counted with Tunstall's herd.

The sun stood a finger's breadth after noon when the drivers started the cattle moving. The bovine river flowed east. A third of the Tunstall men joined the drive. William and Billy stayed back with the other two-thirds to work the ranch.

Repairing the corral, setting fence posts, and cutting wood filled the rest of the afternoon.

Friday. Valentine's Day. William had never sent anyone a valentine. Now he thought of Emily and trembled inside. His palms sweat. "Hoot, hoot," he recited to himself when he imagined seeing her. Only the thought that she was in town and he on the ranch calmed him.

The work of the day before continued—more fence posts, more repairs. William understood the appeal of the life of a ranch hand. There was always something to do, and time never hung heavy. Quiet satisfaction of work well done filled the day, refreshing his spirit like cool water. The company of others whittled away at the bark of isolation that encased him.

Men were meant to be part of a group, he thought, sitting in the glow of the wood-fired stove at night. Not like a wolf pack, in which members constantly sought dominance, but rather part of one larger cooperative of equals—a composite such that the bunkhouse felt like a living thing. He laid his guns on his bed and played chess, moving his rooks with devastating effect, against Billy.

He relaxed. He had survived his first real Valentine's Day. By the next one, he hoped Emily would be his.

The Barbeque

Dawn on Saturday bled in from the eastern sky in streaks of red. William, Billy, and three others saddled for the trip to Lincoln, leaving a scowling, muttering McCloskey behind.

Upon arriving in town, William corralled Sunfish behind the Tunstall store and dropped his tack on the back veranda. As he did, he heard Alex and John in animated conversation through the back door.

"It's going to mean trouble," Alex was saying when William entered.

"You did what you had to," John said. "At least there's no criminal warrant out for you."

Alex stroked his chin, eyes darting around in the unfocused way of deep but rapid thinking. "We need a peace officer on our side," he said at last.

"Spoken like a true solicitor," John laughed. "But the sheriff's position is taken. In fact, all the law-enforcement jobs belong to Dolan's men. How do we get a peace officer of our own?"

Alex winked. "Dolan has never appointed a justice of the peace."

"With a sheriff, one's not needed," John said, fingers absently straightening his lapels.

"We need one," Alex said. "And the fact that a town has a sheriff does not preclude it from also having a justice of the peace."

John squinted, lips pursed. "He would not have much authority."

"He'd still represent the law, and that's authority enough for now."

The door to the back bedroom opened, and Emily came out. She gasped when she saw William, and then said to her brother, "Best I go up front and help Susan. I expect a big day today, lots of trade."

It no longer being Valentine's Day, worry about any romantic expectations Emily had of him was gone. Pleased to be near her again, William watched Emily as he half listened to the conversation around him. Maybe she would have dinner with him, just like she used to in Trinidad. He had a year to figure out where he fit into

Emily's life, and today was a good day for beginnings.

"How about William?" Alex's question snapped William back to the present.

"How about me, what?"

"For justice of the peace," Alex said. "A citizens' committee can appoint one. We'll call a meeting tonight, while we have all these ranchers in town."

"Hoot," William said, left shoulder jerking upward and nearly meeting his ear.

John frowned. "I want William on the ranch. I shall go along with this justice-of-the-peace idea, but I want it to be Dick Brewer."

"Your foreman?"

John nodded, fixing his good eye on William. "He's better known, and no offense, William, a more likely figure of respect. No one calls him a clown."

William shrugged, both shoulders moving smoothly this time. "Not sure I would be c-c-comfortable as a peace officer."

Alex cast a look to his wife, who was ringing up a customer. "I think you'd bring some important skills to the job."

John broke up the discussion by assigning William the task of setting up a place for the citizens' committee to meet.

"How about the Torreon?" William suggested.

"Nobody uses that old place anymore," Alex said. "We could meet out back, behind my house. Plenty of room

75

there. We don't want any of Dolan's men attending. Let's call it a barbeque, make a party out of it. Gives us the right to keep the Dolan men out."

"Would that make it a legal citizens' committee?" John asked.

"Sure. It's not an election; nothing is written about what constitutes a citizens' committee, other than it be a committee of citizens," Alex said in his best courtroom drawl.

John laughed. "I shall let the women know we are having a real knees-up tonight. William, help them set it up. Invite the ranchers who shop with us, but say nothing about it being a citizens' committee. Dolan shall never know what hit him."

"Let's get this barbeque started," Alex said, clapping William on the back.

William found Billy drinking coffee at the hotel. He outlined the plans for the evening.

"I'll round up the rest of the hands," Billy said. "They'll get the food ready. A party for just Tunstall and McSween's friends. Let's you and me keep a close eye on the guest list."

The sky, dark with clouds, planned its own party. The temperature never got out of the forties, and gusts of wind scattered cold droplets—calling cards of guests to come.

Word of the barbeque spread quickly, and the threatening weather failed to dampen the enthusiasm.

Sheriff Brady, making a great show of nonchalance,

strolled up the walk to the McSween house in the afternoon, when the approaching storm seemed most threatening. William met him in front of the veranda.

"Picked a bad day for a cookout," Brady said, jutting his chin toward the billowing cloud bank. "Kind of short notice, wasn't it?"

"Spontaneous," William said.

"Why not wait until next week, then? Hope for better weather."

"A big storm brings people t-t-together," William said, stepping closer to Brady and blocking his view of the house. "No one wants to go home in the coming storm, so John and Alex are feeding their f-f-friends."

"I see, so you're just keeping them out of the weather. Shouldn't be any problem, then, for me and my deputies to join you." Brady shifted his weight as if trying peer around William.

"You want to stay out of the storm tonight, Sheriff? Then just stay home."

Brady nodded, scowling. "I know there's more going on here than a barbeque."

"Yes, Sheriff, there may be d-d-dancing."

Brady scowled and, after one last rubberneck at the barbeque preparations, stomped away.

Guests arrived throughout the late afternoon; they took up stations on the back veranda, where the cold air was infused with the savory smell of cooking meat, lifting spirits in spite of intermittent rain sleeting down. The tiny ice crystals hissed in sizzling destruction as they hit the bed of embers under the slowly turning side of beef.

At seven thirty, platters heaped with sliced and dripping meat called everyone to the McSween dining room. John and Alex circulated among the guests, and William watched the two hold whispered conversations with the male guests. These ended with a nod, or a handshake.

At nine o'clock, as if on cue, the women congregated in the kitchen, while the men retired to the living room. William leaned against the wall near the door, arms folded over his chest.

Alex rapped on a dark wooden table. "I'd like to keep this short. I appreciate you ranchers staying late. With you and the hands from John's ranch, we've got fifteen men here, enough to constitute a committee of citizens."

"What's this about, Alex?" one of the ranchers said as he bit the end off a cigar.

"It's about getting fair law and order around here," Alex said. "It's about getting a peace officer we can trust."

"You running for sheriff?" the cigar man said to general laughter.

"I'm talking about appointing a justice of the peace."

The room quieted.

As Alex outlined the plan discussed that morning, William let his attention drift from the meeting. Had he heard a stealthy footstep on the veranda? With a low whistle, he caught Billy's attention, then wagged his fingers to signal he was going outside.

Billy nodded and glided quietly along the edge of the room to join him. As he passed the window, he stopped to peer out, and then gave a negative shake of his head.

William tiptoed out of the house and onto the veranda. He crept, listening after each step, until he completely circumnavigated the house. Satisfied that no eavesdroppers had slipped by him, he returned to the living room.

"The first time our justice of the peace goes up against the sheriff, it'll start a war," a hawk-faced rancher was saying as William reentered. "Who's going to back him?"

"We all do," Alex said. "We get the law we deserve. We deserve no better than Brady if we're unwilling to fight."

"Look, I'll vote for a justice of the peace," said another, string tie bobbing over a protruding Adam's apple. "But I got a family to watch out for. I'm no gun hand, so count me out of this enforcing business. You think Dick Brewer is tough enough to take on the job?"

"He can appoint his own deputies," Alex said.

"So it *is* a war you're after," the hawk-faced one said.

"A battle is inevitable," Alex said. "Let's not fight it as outlaws."

"Let's not fight it at all," said the cigar man, half his smoke gone.

"Billy McCarty!" Brady's shout from the front yard stopped Alex's reply. "Come out here. I want to talk to ya."

With a look at William, Billy walked to the living room doorway. "What about?" he shouted back.

"I was looking through some handbills. Seems you're wanted in Silver City for questioning, something about a murder."

Susurration swept through the gathered men.

"You mean a killing, but it wasn't no murder," Billy shouted back. "That's an old handbill, put to rest long time ago."

"Maybe, but I still want to talk about it. Come out, or we're coming in."

We? thought William. Best see how many. He slid past Billy and went to the front door, peered out. Eight men stood there, led by Brady. A tall order if shooting started. William stepped onto the veranda, left hand on the butt of his Remington, mentally counting his bullets.

"This is a private party, Sheriff."

"Got a right to come in if Billy don't surrender hisself."

Billy stepped out behind William and moved to his left. "Got a warrant?"

"I'll swear one out now." Brady shifted his weight from foot to foot.

"Takes a judge for that," Alex said from the doorway. "One of you a judge?" He stepped from the house, carrying a lantern, directing its light into the faces of the assembled men.

Brady stepped back, hand shielding his eyes. One by one, as the faces of the others were illuminated, they too stepped back from the light.

William recognized three of them. There was the whip snake–mustachioed man, the rangy cur, and the man with the slithering gun—those who had stood with Brady in John's store on William's first day in town. To these he added four more faces to his mental gallery of rogues.

"As I thought, not a legitimate judge among you," Alex said. "Go back to Dolan, Sheriff; you've got no right to be here."

Shooting guilty looks at each other, the eight men turned and melted into the night.

The clamor when William returned to the living room took some time to die down. The few who hadn't crowded to the window or door to witness the standoff had heard it plainly enough.

"Alex, you were a veritable Diogenes," John laughed. "You certainly did not expect to find an honest man in that crowd, did you?"

"Just shining the light of truth into dark places," Alex laughed back.

"What truth?" William asked.

Alex looked as if he were about to shrug, but the hawk-faced rancher spoke first. "I think this justice-of-the-peace idea might work after all. I say we put it to a vote."

"That truth," Alex said sotto voce.

The motion carried unanimously.

February 18, 1878

The next day William relaxed in his saddle as Sunfish loped toward the Tunstall ranch. The brown hills, which had stood like hieroglyphs above green pastures, were no longer indecipherable. They now promised familiar paths and quiet passages. The Rìo Feliz glistened in the sun, a flowing silver script that read of journey's end.

Billy, uncharacteristically lost in thought, had not made a single jibe. As the ranch house first peeked around a bend in the river, the teenage-faced cowhand edged his horse close to William. "I'm going to change my name," he said.

"Why?" William pulled up slightly on the reins, slowing Sunfish to a trot.

"That handbill thing last night. I shot a man in Silver City over a silly argument. He was armed. Even though it was self-defense, something like that in your past haunts you. Maybe if I change my name, I can leave it behind."

"Maybe. I d-d-doubt it would work for me."

"Only the foolish seek a reputation," Billy went on. "I don't want one. I want to settle down someday."

"On the Tunstall ranch? It is a g-g-good place."

Billy shrugged. "I suppose so. I want to find a gal someplace, make a home with her."

A dream William fully understood. Smiling, he shook his head. "You are young. Plenty of time for that."

"I know, but when I find the right girl, I can't be on the run. So best to change my name now, and leave the sins of Billy McCarty behind."

"What is your new name?" The ranch house was close now, the bunkhouse just the other side of the corral.

"I'm gonna take my mother's name. Bonney. I will be Billy Bonney."

"It fits you. A child's name. You look like a k-k-kid anyway." William's nose wrinkled and his left eye stuttered shut.

Billy kicked William's shin. "And you look like a clown."

They dismounted and busied themselves hitching the horses. Then Billy asked, "What do you want for your future?"

William thought, remembering the first time he was

asked that. "When I first met Jesse, back in Wichita, the sheriff there asked me the same thing."

"Whatja tell him?"

"That I just wanted to find a place where I could be at peace."

"The grave offers that."

"Pretty much what he said."

"Well, you keep on the way you're goin' and you'll find that peace pretty quick."

William smiled at Billy. "I have found the peace I have been looking for, right here. With you and the boys. And Mr. Tunstall." And Emily, he thought but dared not say out loud.

"Here?" Billy laughed. "We're in the middle of a war, Hoots."

"I am at peace inside."

Upon entering the bunkhouse, William saw that many of the hands who had ridden with the Chisum herd had returned from Fort Sumner. New pay jingled in their pockets. Dick Brewer hadn't returned.

The story of the standoff at the barbeque made its rounds, growing in the telling until John Tunstall and his five ranch hands had stood off twenty of Dolan's men in a pitched gun battle.

Brewer rode in Monday morning, and John Tunstall was with him. The foreman had gone straight to Lincoln to turn over the money from the beef contract. William guessed Brewer had been told of his new role as justice of the peace and wondered what he thought of his position. Brewer's deadpan expression gave no clue.

John dismounted and waved William over. "There has been a new development since you left. Last night Brady served me with letters of forfeiture. Alex is lawyering it up so that I can sign most of my assets over to Minnie, putting them out of Dolan's reach for now. She does not want much from the ranch, although I am transferring the deed to her. All she wanted were some horses. We shall round them up today and drive them back tomorrow. I shall take some men back with me, want you to come too."

"Yes, sir," William said, his mood brightening. Then he thought through John's request. "Are you expecting t-t-trouble on the drive? Hoot."

"No. But when I saw you work at the barbeque, I realized you're better positioned in town than out here guarding my depleted herd."

That made good sense, William thought. Been trying to tell him that for two weeks now.

Tuesday, February 18, dawned clear and bright, with round white clouds blowing like tumbleweeds across a prairie sky. The sun climbed well into the heavens as John provided all hands with a hearty breakfast of eggs and cornmeal before setting off with a herd of fourteen horses.

William rode on the left of the herd, letting Sunfish do the work of keeping the horses pointed in the correct direction. McCloskey rode drag, Billy on the right. John and Brewer led the procession riding along the Rìo Feliz until the ranch house lay miles behind.

Eventually John left the river's course and picked his way between the two rounded hills that marked the gateway of the trail to Lincoln.

Billy, riding on the right side and climbing partway up one of the mounds, looked back, and then shaded his eyes with his hand. "Cloud of dust back toward the ranch. Could be riders."

John turned in his saddle. "Billy, turn back with William and McCloskey and see what that is. We shall keep the herd moving forward."

Billy led them back to the river and a mile down its course, and then pulled up. "I'll top that rise there and look ahead," he said, and spurred his horse up a small slope to his left. He raised himself in his saddle, peering from under a shading hand. "Looks like about five riders, heading north across country, away from the river." He shifted to study the direction they were going. "More dust that way. There're more riders coming down the trail toward where we left Mr. Tunstall. We gotta get back!" Billy shouted, spurring his horse away from the river.

William wheeled Sunfish around and galloped back to the mound-marked trail. As he turned Sunfish into that pass, the crack of a gunshot echoed down the hills. Urging his mount to an even faster pace, he rounded a curve and came upon the small herd of horses, now stomping nervously in a huddled group. Billy and Dick were up the trail a few yards, bent over a body in the road.

William rode up and saw it was John Tunstall, shot dead, a revolver in his hand.

For a moment, William struggled with the reverse of his dark tornado. His thoughts spun, but he couldn't move. How could John be dead? The man hadn't owned a gun, but his dead hand held one.

"I saw them," Billy said with a wild look in his eyes. "I saw them—I couldn't get here in time, but I saw them."

"Who were they?" Brewer asked.

Billy looked at William, eyes coming back into focus. "The same ones that stood with Brady at the barbeque."

"Was Brady there?"

"Yes, but he's not the one who killed Mr. Tunstall. Bill Morton shot him, and I saw Frank Baker put a gun in Tunstall's hand after he was shot." Billy ran for his horse. "I'll get those sons of bitches."

"Hold on," Brewer said. "McCloskey, go back to the ranch and get all the riders you can find. Bring them to the Tunstall store. Billy, help me get Mr. Tunstall's body back to town. Then we'll see about this, but we'll do it all legally."

"Legal or not, I'll settle accounts with those that done this." But Billy reined his horse over and dismounted to pick up John's corpse.

William, mouth dry and eyes burning, helped hoist his friend's body over the saddle. A chill ran through him when he thought of Emily getting the news. Numbness gave way to anger. He met Billy's pained look as he finished securing the body. "I am with you, Billy. They will pay."

Largo

They placed John Tunstall's body in the back room of the store. Planks of wood laid across nailed-together packing crates provided a makeshift bier.

Emily, curled into a wan ball, sobbed at his feet.

William stood two paces behind her, head bowed, contemplating mayhem while his right hand first caressed and then retreated from the butt of his holstered Colt. The movements of his hand barely registered; his heart focused on comforting Emily, though there was nothing he could do. When she looked up amid sobs, her spirit seemed as dead as her brother.

"I am very sorry, ma'am," he mumbled, stricken by the accusation in her eyes.

Emily grimaced and, with a sharp shake of her head,

returned to her vigil at John's feet, sobbing anew.

William backed out of the room and closed the door.

Dick Brewer, Billy, and ten hands from the ranch milled about the store's counters, hissing in whispers like steam escaping the boiler of a locomotive.

"Now that Mr. Tunstall's laid out proper," Billy said, "I'm goin' for that murdering Bill Morton."

"You know they're down at the House," Brewer said, using the common name for Dolan's establishment. "Sheriff Brady is there."

"I'll get him too and the rest of his hired killers," Billy said, heading for the door. Several others moved to follow.

"Hold on," Brewer said. "You're going up against the law."

The near-mob stopped in a storm-blow of angry grumbling.

"Hoot. I thought we made you a lawman."

"You did, at that," Brewer said, relief on his face as he fumbled for a pencil. "Anybody got some paper?"

Alex tore a sheet out of the ledger at the front counter and handed it to him. "This do?"

Brewer flattened it on the counter and wrote in a scratchy scrawl. "I'm issuing a warrant for the arrest of Frank Baker and William Morton on the charge of murder." He picked up the lined paper and offered it to Billy. "You gonna serve it?"

Billy grabbed it. "This—and more." He tapped his revolver and whirled on his heel, but William stopped him with a hand on his arm.

"If he is serving a warrant, you had better d-d-deputize him first, Brewer."

"Good idea," Brewer said. "Hold up your hand, Billy."

William raised his as well. "I'll b-b-back you, Billy. For Emily."

After some shifting and glancing around, two of the other Tunstall cowboys raised their hands as well.

With a look of surprise, Brewer swore them in as deputies. "It's official. Go serve the warrants."

"What do we do with Baker and Morton then?" Waite, one of the two hands who had volunteered to be a deputy, asked. "Where we gonna hold 'em?"

Perplexed, Brewer looked at the assemblage. His eyes fell on McSween. "Alex, is there some place at your house where we could lock them up?"

A worried Alex looked around at the grumbling men. "I want those murderers as much as you," Alex said, pulling on his long mustache, "but my wife is there. I don't want my home turned into a shooting gallery."

"Hold them in the T-T-Torreon."

Brewer stroked his chin. "There's the new town jail—the Pit Carcel. Ain't exactly ours to use, but it is nice and handy."

"Won't have to hold them for long," Billy said, his eyes taking on that nutty look that William had noted at their first meeting.

"There'll be no lynching, Billy," Brewer said, enunciating each word fully, eyes locked on Billy's face.

Billy gave no answer and stepped into the street, leading deputies Waite and Jed to the House.

William followed a pace behind. It is his show, William thought, prepared to be just backup. But he also hoped that it came to shooting, for he really wanted to shoot a Dolan man.

Following that train of thought, he hoped Billy knew to draw Morton and Baker into the street. Death waited inside the House for those foolish enough to go in.

No one came out of the two-story building. Billy spit in the street and strode inside.

William's tongue prickled its warning, but he followed. He had promised Billy to back him up, and he never went back on his word.

It was William's first time inside this large building. He took one pace inside and hopped to the right, so he was not backlit against the open door. He waited for his eyes to adjust to the interior shadows.

The spacious room surprised him. Island counters and wall shelving stacked with goods covered an area the size of Tunstall's entire store. The sawn plank flooring stretched away both left and right to doors leading to still other interior rooms.

A center aisle led from the door to the back wall, where a fire crackled behind a stone hearth. Brady conversed with Morton, Baker, and two others near the fireplace. At the entrance of the deputies, the five broke off their discussion and eager grins broke upon their faces. Brady took a step forward, separating himself from the other four and staring hard at Billy.

"Come to turn yourself in?" the sheriff asked, voice mocking.

"Hoot." William took note that one of the two men he did not know startled; the stranger gave him a thorough look.

"Got a warrant here for the arrest of Frank Baker and William Morton for the murder of John Tunstall," Billy said.

William saw that Billy kept moving slowly toward Brady. Trying to close the distance to under ten feet, he thought.

Brady laughed. "You got no warrant. It takes a judge, right?" he mocked.

"And who says it was murder?" Morton said. "Tunstall pulled a gun on us in the performance of our duties."

"I saw Baker put a gun in Tunstall's hand after he'd been shot," Billy said. "You are both under arrest by the authority of the justice of the peace, Dick Brewer. And I reckon the justice of the peace is a judge."

"Justice of the peace?" Brady laughed louder. "I don't recognize any such authority. Now turn over your guns because you're all under arrest."

"I will ensure Brewer's authority is r-r-respected." William touched the butt of his Peacemaker.

"Well, look what the Lord sent me this day," said the gunman William noted earlier. He stepped away from the others and swaggered a couple of steps to stand in front of William.

The other stranger retreated to stand with his back against the stonework of the fireplace, a bemused smile on his face. He looked vaguely familiar, but William couldn't spare him a closer look.

The gunman confronting William wore a tooled black leather gun belt, studded with cartridges. A pearl-handled revolver gleamed in his tied-down holster. The man's face was burnt—brown and cracked with the wrinkles of long days in the sun. His mouth curved in a sneer, though no humor reached the man's calculating eyes.

William recognized the look. The other men standing beside Brady were gunfighters by circumstance; this man was one by choice.

The stranger toyed with the brim of his silver-studded hat. "Heard of a clown like you up in Trinidad."

Brady spoke to William in a satisfied tone, as if he had just said checkmate. "I've seen you a lot around town, but not actually seen you shoot. So you don't scare me none. You're just a fool, playing tough. Today is your day of reckoning. I hear you call yourself William. Just William—no last name, no nickname. Well, meet Largo."

"I disagree," Largo said, dropping his hands so that they hovered over the white butt of his gun. "William here does have a nickname. It's 'clown.' William the Clown."

"Did you know me in Trinidad?"

"Got there too late, but I heard you headed this way. Never expected to find you this easy, though."

"If you think I am easy, you did not spend enough time in Trinidad."

Billy, now within ten feet of Sheriff Brady, stopped moving. "I'll have those guns," he said to Morton and Baker.

Largo smiled, his saffron teeth a sharp contrast to the pearl handles of his gun. "Sheriff Brady, I hear Dolan's hiring men. I'd like to apply. I'll show you my bona fides if William here will be so obliging as to draw."

Brady smiled. "Dolan left for Santa Fe yesterday, but I'm sure he'll hire you."

Largo nodded. "Fair enough. And no need to worry about those papers. I'll take care of the kid there when I'm done with the clown."

"This man is mine," William said to Billy, never taking his eyes off the stranger. Anger at John's murder, rage at the hurt it caused Emily, overwhelmed the warning tickle of his tongue. "Billy, serve those warrants."

The black-belted gunslinger went for his gun. And he was very fast.

Getting the Gang Together

The tornado proved a breeze faster. William's Colt spoke first.

Largo's eyes went wide in surprise, and his pearl-handled gun, already out of its holster, dropped to the floor. William thumbed back his revolver's hammer, ready for a second shot, his eyes scanning Brady and the remaining men.

The barrel of Billy's Thunderer pointed an accusing finger ten inches from Brady's head. The guns of Waite and Jed covered the other three.

William's Colt remained trained on Largo, whose hands were probing the front of his shirt. He puzzled at the blood on his fingertips. Then his eyes rolled back in his head, and he toppled face up on the floor.

"So who was Largo?" William asked Brady. At Brady's scowl, William went through the dead man's pockets. Five hard round objects nestled in an inner vest pocket.

William drew them out and stepped back as if he had found a rattlesnake. He stared at five twenty-dollar gold pieces.

"Let's go," Billy said to Baker and Morton. "Brady, you were there when Tunstall was murdered, but I got no warrant on you this time, so step back."

The third man raised his hands and stepped forward from where he leaned on the stonework of the fireplace. "I wasn't there either."

"I know you, Dick Lloyd. You were riding with the Jesse Evans gang. What're you doing here?"

An icicle plunged into the back of William's throat at the name. Now that he could see Lloyd's face without the obscuring shadow, he recognized him. Scarred cheek, broken nose—the third man when Jesse and Walt had met William in Wichita. The man who had held a gun on Emily at the holdup. "Hoot, hoot, hoot."

"Jesse's gang is with Mr. Dolan now," Sheriff Brady said, though he gave William a funny look. "You're in way over your head, Billy. Lower your gun and go back to Tunstall. Unless you want more funerals."

"Don'tcha worry about that," Billy said. "There's gonna

be more funerals." He motioned to Baker and Morton. "A lot more. Now move."

William, cocked Colt still in his hand, took three deep breaths to steady himself. He waited until Morton and Baker, covered by Billy and the two deputies, were free of the building. He kept his revolver pointed in the general direction of Brady and Lloyd, both of whom stood still and scowling, but showing no inclination to draw. Then William, too, backed out of the building.

The two prisoners and their four guards proceeded down the middle of the street.

They only made it as far as the front of the hotel before seven men materialized from between the buildings on both sides of the street, guns drawn.

"All right, Billy," said one, waving his pistol at Baker and Morton, "let 'em go."

The speaker, a man in his early thirties with a blocky build and dark complexion, wore a hat with a silver-trimmed band. It was Jesse Evans.

The man who had robbed Emily. The man who had fashioned William into a gunfighter. The man who seemed determined to haunt him until the day William died. A cold anger, poised like a bullet in a chamber, formed in his gut. "Hoot, hoot."

Some of the men surrounding them sniggered. Jesse shook his head. "So you've found your way to Lincoln after all, William. Selling your gun again?"

"Jesse," Billy said to the leader, "I left your man Lloyd back at the House. Don't be mixing in here; this is official law business."

Jesse Evans shook his head, smiling broadly. "Morton's a friend of mine too. And according to Sheriff Brady, you are to be arrested on sight."

Billy stepped closer to Morton, poking the barrel of his Thunderer into the base of his prisoner's skull. "Let's see just how good a friend you are of Jesse," he said to his prisoner.

Jesse frowned. "You know me, Billy. I'd just as soon kill you now. Don't think I won't trade Morton—and Baker, too, if it comes to it—for you."

William shifted his weight, picking his targets. Billy and the two prisoners blocked his shot at Jesse. The other two deputies stood between William and three of the surrounding foes. Three men were in the clear—old friends of his. The whip snake–mustachioed man, the rangy cur, and the man with the slithering gun. William saw that his facial tics had drawn their attention. He had five shots left in his Colt.

Morton, hands thrust as high into the air as he could reach, said, "Billy, just let us go and everybody walks away today."

"If it was just me, I wouldn't care about walking away," Billy said. "What do you say, Waite?"

William kept his eyes on the three men in front of him who were growing more restive by the moment. He heard Waite say, "Up to you," but did not see what happened. There was a shot. The men in front of him were grabbing at their guns. The dark tornado blasted in.

Three shots.

Down went the rangy cur, blown backward over his heels.

Down went the whip mustache, spinning in a complete circle as he fell.

Down went the third, his gun blown from his hand and skittering across the barren earth.

William turned on his heel and crouched, sorting out the battlefield.

Waite fired.

Jed, the other deputy, was down.

Smoke billowed from the guns of Dolan's remaining men.

Morton lay on the ground.

Baker down, hands and elbows shielding his head.

Billy fired at Jesse, though he was more than ten feet away.

Jesse fired at Billy.

Then both ran for cover.

William pulled his Remington with his left hand and holstered his Colt with his right.

Waite ducked and tried to grab the fallen deputy with one hand, snap shooting with the other.

William reached him in two quick steps as he transferred the Remington to his right hand. He added his fire to Waite's, five shots so fast they seemed to erupt from a single detonation of gunpowder.

The opposition ducked, interrupting their returning gunfire.

William hooked his left hand under Jed's shoulder and, with Waite's help, pulled him to cover.

Five men lay in the street: Baker, Morton, and the three who had faced William.

Those three lay dead still.

Baker, however, crawled over to Morton, and then the two scuttled to safety near Jesse.

William and Waite half carried, half dragged the deputy the hundred yards to the McSween house, where Alex stood pointing a shotgun down the street.

Dick Brewer and the other men had boiled from the store at the sound of gunfire, and now talked in a great confusion.

"That was a cock-up," Billy said, shaking his head.

"Jed needs a doctor," Waite said. "Somebody get Dr. Woods."

"Before Dolan's men do," Alex said, pointing at the three bodies left in the street.

"They don't need a doctor," Billy said. "Just an undertaker."

"What happened?" Brewer asked Billy.

Billy peered down the street for several moments. Then, apparently satisfied that there was no pursuit, he said, "We arrested Morton and Baker. Jesse Evans interfered."

"Where are Baker and Morton?" Brewer asked, looking now to William.

"Got away," Billy said and spit into the street.

"You had your g-g-gun on Morton."

"Had it pressed right up to his skull," Billy said. "Thought it would intimidate him, keep him from trying anything. But he's a cool customer. He must have felt me relax when I turned to talk to Waite, and he dropped suddenly. Jesse went for his gun and I had to choose quickly, so I shot it out with Evans." Billy grimaced as he rubbed his hands together. "I swear the next time I have Morton and Baker, they're not getting away."

William cleared his head with several deep breaths. Jesse Evans—here, lined up against him again. Well, this time William was no untried kid. He looked forward to the encounter.

He felt something heavy in his breast pocket and patted the coins there. That reminded him of the stranger dead in Dolan's parlor. What did his arrival mean?

"Who was Largo?" he asked Billy.

"I've not seen him around here before," Billy said. "Not part of the Evans gang, so far as I know. Just a drifter for hire, a running gun, passing through and looking for work."

Holding up one of the gold coins, William said, "He was more than just a drifter. He had work. But in whose p-p-pay?"

Funeral

r. Woods arrived, and several men helped carry Jed into the McSween house. Brewer called the remaining men back into the Tunstall store.

"Dolan's got the Jesse Evans gang with him, and soon they'll all be sporting deputy badges," Brewer said. "I'm going to deputize anyone here who wants to regulate the law."

Everyone in the room raised their hands and took the oath. Brewer said, "Your first task as Regulators is to bring in the posse that killed Mr. Tunstall. Start with Morton and Baker."

"Everyone in the posse? Brady was there," Billy said.

"I know. I was there with you," Brewer said. "Everyone."

The Wortley Hotel was too close to Dolan's territory to make it a safe headquarters, so the Regulators stayed farther down the street at the Courthouse Saloon and at the Montano boardinghouse and bordello, which was separated from the saloon by Squire Wilson's office. As news of the shootings spread and additional men came to join the Regulators, they found bunk space at the Ellis house and gristmill, which occupied the easternmost parcel of land in Lincoln.

Lincoln's jail, less than a year old, was a hole with the jailer's quarters built over a trapdoor that led down to the log-lined cell, called the Pit Carcel. The McSween faction's positions now surrounded it on three sides, making it a better holding area than the Torreón.

William was happy about that, for the Torreón became his home. He left the meeting, now a bona fide Regulator, and climbed the wooden steps to the upper floor of his private quarters. He had tried to see Emily, but she remained shuttered within the private room at the store. He heard her weeping through the closed door. Poor woman, he thought. Let her grieve tonight. He knew he would.

William tossed fitfully on the rough wooden planking of the Torreón. An aching hollowness made sleep elude him. The sharp edges of grief refused to smooth into slumber. Did he fear dreaming of an accusatory John or did he damn himself for letting John die? At last his tired mind could hold out no longer and sleep claimed him.

He did not dream of John. He dreamt of Emily wearing a striped silken dance-hall costume and performing on a rough stage lit by flickering torches. The crowd of men hooted and hollered. One man, his right eye hidden by a black patch, threw pieces of gold at Emily's feet. She stooped to pick one up, then fled from the stage. William chased after her, but she had disappeared out the back door, leaving a discarded dance-hall dress.

Eyes burning from too little sleep, William met Billy and Brewer the next morning at the Tunstall store. Billy was eager to march down to the House again and take Morton and Baker, and Brady too.

"Jed's still with Doctor Woods," Brewer said. "And we have Mr. Tunstall's funeral to prepare. Let's take a few days to lick our wounds."

"Gives Brady the same time to lick his," Billy said. "We came out on top last night; I say we press him hard now. Time plays into his hands more'n ours."

That made sense to William, but his thoughts turned to Emily. She needed her brother's friends around her now—not off chasing rogues around the countryside. Sure, those responsible would pay, but a few days wouldn't make that much difference. He faced Billy. "I will wait until after John's—Mr. Tunstall's f-f-funeral. Out of respect for Miss Tunstall."

"She'd feel better if her brother's murderers were punished," Billy said.

"They will be. Hoot. After the funeral."

"Get all the hands together," Brewer said, his tone between a sigh and command. There was steel in his watering eyes. "We got a funeral to plan, and a few other things besides."

*   *   *

Two days later, John Tunstall's funeral was held at the safer venue of Fort Sumner. William stood at the graveside, head bowed, watching Emily from the corner of his eyes.

Her face was drawn and haggard, her lips pressed together in a tight line. She winced when Alex dropped the first shovelful of dirt. It thumped upon the coffin in a gravelly drumbeat.

William shifted his feet, inching in Emily's direction. She seemed on the edge of collapse, he thought, likely to faint right into the grave. Though Susan, a runnel of tears on her cheek, stood by her side, William doubted she'd be able to catch Emily if she dropped.

He glanced at the other men in attendance. They stared into the grave, faces tight vignettes of anger, sorrow, and confusion.

Pain suffused Billy's features, and he ground his teeth. Sniffing, he rubbed the heel of his hand across the bridge of his nose.

Dick Brewer stood as still as a grave marker, fingers clenched into gargoyle claws.

McNab, a Tunstall cowhand, glanced back and forth from Billy to Brewer, unable to fix on anything.

The Coe brothers hid their faces, sobbing.

Susan stood at Emily's side, holding her hands, hugging her shoulders, patting her back.

William edged closer to Emily. It was proper that Susan, Emily's only female friend, support her in this time of mourning. He knew they shared many secrets and lent strength to one another, and Emily had never needed strength more than today. He did not want to intrude, but he held himself at the ready.

The gravediggers took up their shovels to complete the worst and final moments of the funeral. They worked as quickly as respect allowed, their rhythmic cadence playing a dirt dirge.

More color drained from Emily's face with each measure of earth thrown down onto the coffin. She did not move until the last pat of shovel shaped the mound her brother lay beneath. Then she fell upon the grave in a half swoon, half last embrace.

Susan bent to comfort her.

William hovered within reach, but not touching either woman, fighting to suppress his tics.

Billy ground his teeth, fists clenched, and a spasm of pain crossed his face as if he had been punched in the ribs. He lifted his bowed head to look at the others, his eyes flashing. "I'll get every son of a bitch who helped kill John if it's the last thing I do."

A chorus rose in angry agreement.

Brewer held up his hand for quiet. "There's a federal marshal here in Fort Sumner. His name on arrest warrants can get us Morton and Baker, in spite of what Brady does."

"Let's get Brady too while we're at it," Billy said.

"I will meet you at the marshal's office," William said, thinking his business with Emily was not yet finished.

The men walked past the church and toward town. McSween, at Brewer's shoulder, talked rapidly while striking the palm of one hand with the index finger of his other as he made some lawyerly point.

William lingered, sad eyes on Emily. When Susan took her by the arm and led her from the graveside, he followed into a shadowy, rough-hewn church similar to the one he had attended as a boy. The absence of an apse or font declared this a Protestant church, though not distinguishing whether Methodist or Lutheran or some other affiliation. William had heard that back east the various Protestant sects had separate churches, the faithful preferring to worship with like-minded folk. It made no difference to William; he was always a church of one. Reverend Hawkins would have thought that was pride. Not pride, William thought. Anger.

The church was small—only five rows of pews. The chill air within remained unwarmed by the ray of sunlight that fingered through the air to sit reverently on the minister's lectern. The empty cross adorning the pulpit gleamed silver in its light.

Emily sat in shadow, Susan beside her in quiet grief.

William studied the cross, which radiated a halo in the slender beam. Hope? he wondered. Reunion after the grave? John was dead. Where was the solace for the living? He watched Emily as she teetered on the brink of despair. What good was the shining cross for Emily now as she sat staring blindly at her feet?

William opened the mental saddlebag where he carried his religious training. He asked the same question he had as a boy while sitting at the back of the church—and as an adult in the saloons, where he brooded at lonely tables. Why is God so cruel? Or is he just careless?

These questions had spiked him for years, and he hung limp after so many cruel nails. He thought himself numb to further outrage. But, he believed this might be the first time Emily had confronted the pain of an uncaring God. Alone.

One last chance, God. Was there a reason that God had brought him here? Let it be to lend Emily strength.

Wyatt Earp had told him he would find a place of peace. That was three years ago, and still he searched. All he had found was trouble, escalating from tragic misunderstandings to two factional wars in as many months.

Peace was not something found, like a green valley or a cool spring. Peace had to be torn from a harsh land. The Trinidad sheriff had reminded him that William's kind did not make friends. He would prove the man wrong. He would find a center, surround himself with friends, and take a stand. At this time. With these people.

And if his rascal God objected, then let him be clear.

Broken People

As if she divined his thoughts, Emily looked up at him at that moment of his reflection. "It is very kind of you to stay with me, William. But you should join Brewer and the others."

"I will as soon as I am sure there is nothing I can d-d-do for you."

Emily put her hands over her eyes. "Half of me is torn away. I do not recognize my own life. You led me through the mountains, but this is a wilderness you cannot help me cross."

"We are both broken people." William nodded past the salty taste of tears on his tongue. "If I could just b-b-bear some of the burden for you."

"How could you?" Emily's hands snapped to her sides; her eyes burned with a touch of madness. "Has darkness ever trapped you so that you knew, deep in your soul, that it was never, ever going to get better? I have lost my brother forever, and he isn't coming back. 'Out, out, brief candle . . .' You have strutted and fretted your 'hour upon the stage,' and I shall hear you 'no more.'"

"I stood in darkness," William said. "I started walking. Find the light, Emily, and walk towards it." He stopped his tongue, though his thoughts continued. Let me be your light.

Emily drew back, frowning, her eyes once again wells of sadness. "'Everyone can master grief but she who has it.' I shall not return to Lincoln. But Susan and the others shall. Go back with them, William."

William shivered in ghostly premonition. "Where will you go?"

"This western frontier has too little law. I will follow your advice and walk towards the light. I shall return to England, where the light of civilization does not dim. 'He that dies pays all debts.' I will throw myself on my father's mercy, and beg his forgiveness."

Susan raised her bowed head to look sharply at Emily, lips pursed as if in warning.

Confused, William asked, "Forgiveness for what?"

"For coming west in the first place," Emily said, words flowing like a spring-thawed brook. "John thought we needed a place where a man's potential was not limited by family, where he could make his own way and by his own rules."

"Do you think your father will blame you for your brother's d-d-death?"

"Maybe, partly, but John and I were in his disfavor before now."

"Then stay here. Why add one wound on top of another?"

"I must heal, and I need my father's blessing to do so." Emily cast her eyes downward at her hands folded in her lap.

"Emily, when it comes to blessings, you already have mine."

Emily looked up and a sigh escaped her. She stood and took William's hand, and led him to another pew, away from Susan. "I must tell you something, William. When you have heard it, you will not want to travel any farther with me. But if you can find any pity in your heart, I ask that you return to Lincoln and avenge John's death."

"I swear vengeance for John. And not for pity, but because he was noble and g-g-good."

Emily shook her head, and her voice dropped to a quivering whisper. "John loved me more than was seemly for a sister." Her face colored a dark red.

William stared. "You mean you and he . . . ? By your consent?"

She seemed to shrink before him. "Yes," she mumbled.

Her word cut through William like a bushwhacker's bullet, scattering all thoughts. Stricken, he sank to a pew, while an emotional cyclone scattered a detritus of long-held hopes and newly minted dreams. Doubt about everything he had ever held to be true assailed him. Vulnerable, he reached inside for something to grasp, some inner strength. His heart crawled back into its coffin. He screwed his emotions down tight. He put on his gunfighter face.

William ran a mental finger over his innermost feelings where, until just moments before, Emily had taken up residence and now found a raw gouge. His keenness for Emily collapsed as dead as her brother. His darkest certainty churned to the surface: Death in all its forms comes quick and unexpected, for a gunfighter more than most. He shivered at the thought. Impassively he searched her face, now partially turned from him, eyes not meeting his. He thought of their trip over the Raton, realizing the frozen rock that stood between them now had no clear pass.

He had wanted clarity from God. Well, now he had it. Emily was not the center he sought. He'd been playing a dead hand all along. All that was left was his code: to be true to his word and fair in his actions. He had promised Emily service and protection. If she asked him to be her avenger, then he would. He would chase down those who killed her brother. He would be a wind of vengeance. For John, for Emily, and for his own broken dream.

William rose from the pew and looked at Emily, who stood in a shroud of shadow. "I will avenge John," he said. He waited for two heartbeats. "Miss Tunstall."

A flash of deep pain crossed her face. She nodded her head stiffly, and her eyes closed in utter despair.

So be it, he thought. And that goes for you too, God.

Marshal McAdams

William left the church and sought Alex and the others. His chest felt empty, a hollow aimlessness that did not pass even when he found the marshal's office.

In the office, Alex remonstrated with Marshal McAdams. All the Tunstall men were there but none of the other mourners. A locked rack of rifles hung by the door; an iron potbellied stove squatted in one corner, its flue snaking up through two elbow bends. Floorboards bowed beneath a large desk that took up one long wall. A door opposite the desk was bound in metal with an iron grate at eye level. The acrid smell of urine drifted from beyond the bars.

McAdams sat in his chair behind the desk, and its wheels squeaked when he shifted position. Middle-aged, with a weather-beaten face that sagged in early jowls, the marshal gazed intently at Alex while scrawling notes on a lined pad.

"So for those reasons I want you to issue a warrant for the arrest of William J. Brady, William Morton, and Frank Baker," Alex said, leaning on the edge of McAdams's desk.

McAdams nodded and leaned back in his chair. "Do you have anything on Dolan?"

"Nothing we can press in court, but he's behind all this," Alex said.

"Warrants for those three without settling Dolan won't do you much good," McAdams said. "Now if you had something on him, we'd be talking. I've been trying to break up that Santa Fe gang for years now."

"The Santa Fe gang?" Brewer asked, looking from Alex to McAdams and back.

"A gang of crooks that runs the territory," McAdams said. "Dolan's in with them, but there's others. Territorial politics are infested with them, Governor Axtell included."

"I knew that Dolan was tight with the governor," Alex said, "but not as coconspirators in a criminal enterprise." He looked at Brewer with his pupils bobbing yolk-like on the whites of his eyes. "The governor could call out the militia against us."

"Not only that," McAdams continued, "I suspect that Colonel Nathan Dudley, the Fort Sumner commander, has been suborned by them as well. If so, he could bring the army in on Dolan's side."

"What have we gone up against?" Brewer asked, his voice dry and raspy.

"You've got a tiger by the tail, no doubt," McAdams said. "Of course, if I'm able to prove Colonel Dudley is actively involved, I can have him removed. On the other hand, he is due for retirement in six months."

"Then Dolan is sure to make his move soon," Alex said, "while he can still count on the army's support if needed."

McAdams leaned back in his chair, metal wheels protesting the shift in weight. "I hadn't considered that angle," he said. "All right. I'll give you all the warrants you need to shake this thing lose. What were those names again?"

Billy listed all the men he had recognized in the posse that killed Tunstall.

"Better add Jesse Evans and his g-g-gang. We will be shooting it out with them before l-l-long."

McAdams looked up from his papers and gave William a wry look. "Can't really issue a warrant before the crime has been committed."

"Just write down attempted m-m-murder. It will be true enough."

"Anything else?" McAdams asked with a harrumph and a grin.

"Something to get us out of j-j-jail if needed."

Alex raised his hand, index finger pointing upward. "A federal writ of habeas corpus, three or four of 'em." He looked at William. "Good thinking."

Though McAdams scratched out each warrant quickly, using a pen which he slashed into the inkwell on his desk repeatedly, it was after three by the clock on his wall when all the papers had been signed. Finished, the marshal leaned back in his chair, hands clasped behind his head. "When will you be returning to Lincoln?"

"Right now, of course," Billy said. "I mean to get to Morton and Baker by midnight. Seems fitting that we take 'em on the same day as Mr. Tunstall's funeral."

Brewer raised his hands shoulder height, fingers spread, and faced Billy. "Hold on. Let's get organized first."

"We got these federal warrants. How much more organized can you get?"

"I'm just the justice of the peace," Brewer said, "and Brady has already said he doesn't recognize my authority. It'll take plenty of men to convince him otherwise."

"These are federal warrants. Certainly he'll recognize that authority," McAdams said, unclasping his hands and making the chair squeak as he leaned forward.

"He's not going to sit idly by while we arrest him," Brewer said. "The papers make the job legal, but they don't get it done."

"Hoot," William said, drawing a curious look from Marshal McAdams. "He has the Evans gang, and that makes for a lot of d-d-deputies on his side."

McAdams drummed his fingers on the desktop. "Suppose I appoint someone in Lincoln with federal powers."

"Doesn't it take a judge to do that?" Alex asked.

"No more so than issuing federal arrest warrants and writs of habeas corpus. But seeing as there's no judge, I've been granted the power to do those things. Of course, my decisions are reviewed and certified by the circuit judge when he has time, but for now, my word is the law."

Alex pursed his lips for a moment and nodded. "Pretty much the same setup as Lincoln, though there the circuit judge never seems to arrive. Who would you appoint?"

"An honest and trustworthy man well known to me. Squire Wilson."

"I know him, of course," Alex said. "He lives across the street from the Tunstall store. But he's not a Regulator."

"Good," McAdams said. "Even more reason to trust his judgment in these matters." He set down his pen, reached into a desk drawer, and withdrew a page of parchment bordered with swirls of ink like eagles in flight. The seal of the United States crowned the top. From another drawer he retrieved an old-fashioned goose-feather quill. "I will appoint Squire Wilson town constable."

McAdams dipped the quill in the inkwell and slowly

filled out the certificate. He rocked a blotter upon the finished product with a self-satisfied sigh. Handing it to Brewer, he said, "Have Wilson swear you in as justice of the peace once you give him this certificate. That should solidify your claim to the office."

"Very nice, I'm sure," Billy said, picking up several of the warrants. "Now can we go?"

"I'm not returning to Lincoln today," Alex said. "I'm staying with Susan until she gets Miss Tunstall settled here in Fort Sumner. It's too late to get to Lincoln before dark."

"Don't care. I'll ride all night if I have to." Billy's face was set like stone, his tone unyielding.

Alex turned to William. "How about you? Staying the night?"

A moment of sadness passed over William. "I am not needed here. I will r-r-ride with Billy."

McNab and the Coe brothers threw in with Billy and left the marshal's office to retrieve their horses.

"I'll stay here in Fort Sumner with Alex so we can ride back together. No one should ride alone now." Brewer's eyes narrowed as he looked at Billy. "Don't do anything until I talk with Squire Wilson and he swears me in as justice of the peace."

"No promises. Best hurry along." Billy folded the warrants for Brady, Morton, and Baker and stuck them inside his shirt.

The sun had long set, and William's four riders were still ten miles from Lincoln. Billy had pushed them on at first but at dark had slowed the pace under the diamond-white stars.

"We got three men to arrest," Billy said. "I say we manage it one murderer at a time."

"That leaves t-t-two more on the outside, warned and ready."

"We'll get Brady first, tonight. With him locked away, Morton and Baker won't have any warning, and we'll get them first thing tomorrow."

"Alex said to wait until he t-t-talks to Squire Wilson."

"I hate standing around, waitin'," Billy said, and spit. "Alex won't be back till afternoon tomorrow at the earliest."

"Brady is not expecting anything, unless we t-t-tip our hand too early. Once we have Squire Wilson's blessing, we can take ten of the Regulators and arrest all three at once. Hoot. Nice and neat."

Billy scowled off into the darkness, but did not say anything.

They finished their ride in the dark and, once in town, went their separate ways. William walked Sunfish to the corral. He brushed the horse and tended to the rick, making sure it was filled with hay. The Tunstall store, unlit tonight, a dark shadow just up the slope from the corral, stirred a feeling of loss in him, an emptiness that grew with each memory of this place.

Bedroll in hand, he went to the Torreón, glad to see the end of the day.

The House

The next morning dawned in the fiery red warning of a storm to come. William stretched in the cold air and blew on his hands, wreathing them in vapor. He wanted hot coffee, but the Tunstall store was closed and no one was home at the McSweens'. He walked across the street, checked westward toward the House. No one was about. He turned to squint into the rising sun. A few of the Regulators were moving about the Montano boardinghouse.

When William entered the building, he found Billy and McCloskey arguing. William poured himself a tin cup of steaming coffee. Warmth limbered his fingers.

"I have warrants right here," Billy said, waving a rolled paper in McCloskey's face.

"I'm just saying to wait until there's a few more of us," McCloskey said. "Or at least till Alex gets back."

"Bah, there's enough of us here now. Me an' William and George Coe there. McNab there, couple of you others—that's all we need."

"It is pretty early. Are you sure they are at the House? Got to g-g-get all three rats in one trap, or they will scatter."

"See there, Billy? Listen to William," McCloskey said. "I'll just go down to Wortley's for breakfast and look around, see if'n anyone's there."

"Sure, got a good view of the House from there," Frank Coe said. "How about it, Billy? Just to be sure?"

Billy frowned, turning his upper lip white. He snapped at McCloskey. "And if you don't see anything, why don't you just go on in the House and look around?"

"Don't worry, I won't tip our hand." McCloskey set down his coffee cup and stretched. "I'll go see about that breakfast."

After McCloskey left, William asked Billy, "You have a p-p-problem with McCloskey?"

"Maybe." Billy drew his Thunderer and checked the chambers. "He and Baker used to ride together."

"So?" McNab said. "You used to ride with the Jesse Evans gang." He smiled and pointed at the gun Billy was holding. "But you're an ironclad Regulator now."

William's tongue hinted at a tingle. "You rode with Jesse Evans?"

"Couple o' years back, before Mr. Tunstall hired me. Jesse started rustlin' and I left." Billy sighed and put his gun away. "If he were lined up with us, we'd get along okay. But Jesse's picked the wrong side, and I'll take him down with Brady."

A couple of years ago? William thought. Must be just after he had met Jesse in Wichita. So Jesse had gone to New Mexico when William went on to the mining towns of Colorado. But Billy having ridden with Jesse might be a plus.

To Billy he said, "Then you know how he thinks, what to expect of him."

"I guess, if you ever really know how any man thinks," Billy said. He glanced at the wall clock.

An hour passed while Billy paced the room and stared frequently at the clock. Several times he went to the door and looked up and down the street. Finally, Billy hitched at his gun belt. "That's long enough for waitin'. I'm going to the House now; anyone comin' with me?"

"We should wait for Alex. Hoot. But I will g-g-go with you if you mean to go now."

McNab and Coe, fidgeting with their holstered sidearms, stepped forward as well. The four men went out into the brisk February air. They marched down the dirt street, their shadows stretched out before them.

McCloskey came out of the Wortley Hotel as they passed and joined them. "Didn't see anyone," he said.

"They're in there," Billy said, turning to face the House. "Where else would they be? Frank, you watch this side."

McNab stopped and faced the building, an eye on the east-side exit.

"George, you watch the other side," Billy said, and Coe took up position on the west.

"I'll stay back a piece and watch the balcony," McCloskey said, pointing to the long second-floor veranda that overhung the front door.

Billy squinted a brief look of doubt at William and indicated McCloskey with a roll of his eyes. Then he took a deep breath and shoved open the front door.

Several shoppers looked up, startled at the door's explosive opening, and drew back. The room hung silent until a pop from a burning log broke the spell. Billy whirled at the sound. Baker, Morton, and Brady were not there.

"Where's Sheriff Brady?" Billy asked the room in general. "Where are Morton and Baker?" He glared around.

The people there stood quietly, stiff and hunched, as if trying to be invisible. Finally, the clerk pointed a shaky finger at the side door to William's right.

"Watch 'em," Billy said. He strode to the door and pulled it open. The room beyond held a pool table, and Brady was standing by one corner, chalking a cue.

"You want something, Billy?"

Billy, eyebrows moving upward in unspoken question, shot a quick look over his shoulder at William.

William studied the men still standing stiffly in the store. None met his gaze, and William knew that those wearing guns wished they weren't. "Anyone not looking for t-t-trouble, leave now."

The store cleared out in moments, including the clerk. William turned back to Billy. "All clear in the store." He joined Billy in the pool parlor.

"Well." Brady studied the chalked end of the stick. "What can I do for you?"

"You can tell me where Baker and Morton are," Billy said, hand near the butt of his gun. "And then you can come with us. You're under arrest."

Brady sighed. "Not this again. I don't hold with any chicken scrawls you got, even if they are from a federal marshal. As Alex pointed out at the barbeque, takes a judge to issue a warrant."

"These warrants are good enough for me," Billy said. "I say they give me legal cause to shoot you if you resist. Now where are Baker and Morton?"

Brady stopped fiddling with the pool cue and looked steadily at Billy's hand, which hovered near his Thunderer. A sheen of sweat bathed the sheriff's brow. He looked at William and his face paled. "Baker, Morton, Jesse, and a couple of Jesse's men left town this morning."

Billy cursed. "Going where?"

"West. I think."

"Put down the cue and come with us," Billy said, drawing his gun. "Your pool-playing days are over."

"What are you going to do?" Brady's voice cracked when he spoke. "Are you gonna kill me?"

"Not today, if you come quietly. If not . . ." Billy finished his sentence by pointing his gun at Brady's heart and cocking the hammer.

Brady Goes

Brady raised his hands. "Okay, I'll go, 'cuz you've got the gun on me this time. But I won't be stayin' long, and next time, I'll be the one with the gun."

Billy's eyes went nutty. His hand trembled.

William drew his Colt and aimed it at Brady. "No, Billy. I have Brady covered. Put your gun away. And you, Brady, do not say another word."

With a brittle-ice stare, Billy holstered his gun. "I want you to die slow," he growled into Brady's face. "I want you to hang."

They marched a docile Brady to the Pit Carcel without interference from any of Jesse's men. Once there, Brady climbed down the wooden ladder, and the trapdoor was locked above him.

William and the four other deputies returned to the Montano boardinghouse.

"I'm going after Morton and Baker," Billy said. "They never would have gotten away if it weren't for all this lollygagging and waiting around."

"I'll go with you, b-b-but after Alex gets here."

"I'm in, but I agree with William," McNab said. "When Alex returns, we can provision at the Tunstall store. Then we'll run them down."

Billy swore and stomped out. He unhitched his horse and—with short, sharp movements—mounted, aimed the horse west, and galloped off.

A storm blew in at midafternoon and dumped a few inches of snow. William noted that Alex and Susan hadn't yet returned. Dick Brewer was missing, presumably still with Alex. Equally as worrisome, Baker and Morton were unaccounted for, and Jesse and his gang gone as well.

Most of all, he worried about Billy. Riding after Baker and Morton alone was foolish, no matter how good a shot Billy was at ten feet. Maybe he should have gone with Billy, but William had experience with the fury of winter storms and the dangers to ill-prepared travelers.

And then there was the storm brewing in Billy himself—those nutty eyes signaling the trampling of Billy's reasoning by the stampede of his emotions. Storm within, storm without—no matter; Billy, in his own way, was as dangerous as William's dark tornado.

The sun's position, diffused behind the clouds, could only be discerned by a fading glow that sank in the west. The temperature dropped steadily. William shivered.

The week that had started with such promise at the barbeque had failed. What was it? Friday? Saturday? He had started out the week with the three best friends of his life.

John—dead.

Emily—gone.

And now Billy? What if Billy did not return? William had promised Emily to avenge John's death. But if Billy were also lost, could he do it? Could he bear to be completely alone again in this world? He thought the pain of it would drive him on, out of New Mexico, maybe to the big lonely they called Texas.

Billy returned just after sundown in a good mood. He asked Señor Montano for a plate of beans and spoke between mouthfuls of the spicy black ragout. "I cut their trail where they left the road and headed north cross-country. Couldn't track 'em far after that 'cuz it started snowing."

"How far do you think they g-g-got?"

"Not far. They were headed toward the black-river country, but the snow probably drove them to shelter for the night. If we leave before sunup and cut across country from here, we can catch 'em before noon tomorrow."

"Alex is not b-b-back yet."

"Then I guess he and Brewer'll miss the fun," Billy said. "Probably better that way. This is a job for real riders, not some lawyer. No offense to Alex."

William couldn't argue that point, but thought they would miss having Brewer along. "Hope I do not slow you d-d-down any."

"You'll do fine," Billy said, and he pushed away his empty plate. "Just leave the tracking to the Coe brothers."

"Brewer ought to be with us when we catch up to Morton and his skunks. Any word you can leave him as to where to j-j-join us?"

McNab laughed. "I guess you don't get the notion of tracking."

Black River

illy thought for a moment. "Jesse used to have a hideout in the black-river country. We should catch them somewhere along the Rio Penasco—provided, of course, they're not heading all the way to Santa Fe."

"Leave Brewer a n-n-note. Tell him to meet us there and to l-l-leave Alex here to settle things with Squire Wilson and look after Brady." William yawned and stretched. "I will turn in. Early day tomorrow, and my horse needs t-t-tending."

Before dawn the next day, William joined with the others in front of the Montano boardinghouse. McNab, promising to bring Brewer and supplies to the Río Peñasco hideout once the Tunstall store opened, stayed behind. McCloskey took McNab's place so that Billy led four riders into the valley west of town.

In less than a mile, Billy turned them from the road, cutting toward the northwest.

William could only think of the cold. He wanted to hold the collar of his leather duster closed with one hand, but kept them both on the reins. It was big country, and Billy pushed them without pause.

The task William had undertaken when he swore to avenge John's death swelled in proportion to the landscape. He knew he was no tracker. If not for Billy, he would already be lost—a cold, dark mote on the swell of rolling hills.

In a way, without really thinking about it, William had entrusted his life to Billy. The realization sent shivers, and not from the cold, chasing across his neck and shoulders. He took a deep breath, let his tongue relax in his mouth. There was no itch-quiver to it. Perhaps he was safe in Billy's hands. But there was something unsettling about those nutty eyes.

He questioned if he trusted Billy. It wasn't his physical health that worried him. It was deeper—could William trust Billy with his soul? Without trust, there were no friends. But with trust, there was danger, exposure. Did William truly want to give up the solitary life? Could he let down his guard even that much?

The wind whipped up at times, and the blowing snow turned the rider in front of William into a ghostly blur. He knew that if he became separated, he would die. He glanced at the ground in front of him; the tracks of the leading horses filled quickly with snow.

He looked back up. He was alone. Panic beat at him. Beneath him, Sunfish plodded steadily forward. Was his horse following the correct path? Or should he stop before wandering too far off course? An agony of choice burned within him.

And still, Sunfish plodded on, an unhesitating forward roll of shoulders and haunches.

William bet on trust and let Sunfish have his head.

The wind died down, and as the swirling snow settled, William saw McCloskey ahead of him, shoulders slumped against the cold, following Billy's lead.

As Billy had promised, they struck the Río Peñasco before noon. He led them along its tree-lined, serpentine banks until they reached a small grove of juniper trees beneath an overhang of rock. A small stream of black water flowed through the stand of trees to join the river.

Following Billy into the grove, William entered a small space cleared of trees in the center.

Billy dismounted. "We'll make this our base camp and fan out from here," he said. He motioned to the top of the rocky wall. "McCloskey, stand guard up there while the rest of us look around."

"It's cold up there. I'm gonna want a fire," McCloskey said.

Billy spat. "That would be just plain stupid, unless you want Jesse to know we're here."

"What makes you think he don't?" McCloskey cupped his hands and blew into them. "He surely knows about this little grove. He's probably been watchin' us for the past couple of miles."

"Stop arguin' and git up there."

McCloskey muttered a few words under his breath, but he started to climb.

"Is this Jesse's old h-h-hideout?"

"No, but his hideout's close by," Billy said. "This is where I told Brewer to meet us." He waited for McCloskey to work his way to the top of the rock. "Follow me and keep your eyes open," he said and turned his horse away from the river.

William followed and thought how McCloskey had looked like a spider as he crawled up to his watch post. William tried to keep track of the way back to the watered grove, but the twisting trail that Billy led them on made it impossible to think of it as anything more than "back there."

He revisited his previous misgivings about putting his life in Billy's hands. Not that he didn't trust the kid, but what if something happened to Billy? They were riding against a gang of outlaws led by a notorious killer. They could be bushwhacked. Billy could be killed in a duel with

Jesse. There were many ways William could be separated from the others, and left alone on the cold tundra, lost.

Sunfish chuffed and shook his head, breath steaming. William relaxed; Sunfish could find the way home.

William's thoughts snapped back to the present when Billy raised a warning hand and pulled up. Through the trees ahead, he saw a rough cabin, three unsaddled horses tethered to a post in front, and a curl of smoke from the chimney.

Capture

Billy drew his gun and motioned them ahead. His horse had taken only a few steps when the cabin door opened and Baker stepped out.

Baker saw Billy, yelped, and ducked back inside. Gunfire erupted from the cabin, making Billy jump for the trees.

William rode Sunfish, circling to his right, through the cover of the woods until he was certain that his horse was out of the line of fire. After dismounting, he tied the reins loosely around a low branch. He drew his Remington and peered around the trunk of an oak. A pall of blue gun smoke drifted over the cabin, but there were no clear targets.

That didn't stop Billy, though, as he fired into the cabin. "You're trapped. Throw out your guns and come out," he yelled. "Or we'll burn you out."

The shots from the cabin diminished. They must be thinking it over, William thought. Now was the time to get into a better position. He worked himself to his right to cover the rear of the hideout. He saw a lean-to in back of the cabin, and three saddled horse were tethered to low pine branches. With the three in front, that made six. Why six horses?

Remounts! He gave away his position to shout, "Billy, they have three fresh horses in the b-b-back, saddled and ready."

As if on cue, a sudden commotion of pounding feet and neighing horses behind the cabin signaled the escape of its occupants. Three men ran for the waiting horses.

William snap fired at them.

One fell.

The two others vaulted into their saddles and pounded through the brush, out of sight.

William ran back to Sunfish. He leapt onto his saddle and set off in pursuit. Behind the cabin he found a narrow track worn through the underbrush. He urged Sunfish along it, his Remington still in his hand. A gunshot on his left marked the emergence of Billy crashing out of the woods in similar pursuit.

The woods opened up to reveal an undulating plain beyond. William spied the two fleeing men, already dark disappearing specks against the white open land.

Billy spurred his horse and pulled ahead of William. Shouts from behind told him the rest of the posse was catching up.

William realized he was not the horseman his companions were. Though he rode as fast as he could, his companions rode at a smoother gait, more balanced, their horses fleeter. William soon found himself bringing up the rear. Flashes of fire and puffs of smoke ahead reported the ongoing exchange of fire between the fugitives and their pursuers.

Billy's horse was the fastest of all, or carried the lightest load, for he slowly overtook the two wanted men, forcing them to veer away from him in a wide arc to William's right.

William stopped chasing the fleeing men and adjusted Sunfish's direction. He picked a spot on the men's curved course and raced the fugitives to it. In some ways, it was like herding cattle, all at a body-pounding pace.

Their quarry began to string out. The hindmost one called out for help. His partner dropped back and circled up. When William arrived, Morton and Baker had their guns pointed into the air, unwilling to relinquish them entirely.

Billy and the Coe brothers hemmed them in.

"We surrender," Morton said, "if you promise you'll take us back to Lincoln alive."

Billy bit his lower lip as he studied the two prisoners. "Drop your guns to the ground."

William kept his revolver loosely trained on Morton. "Do you really have a choice?"

Baker gave him a dark look. "You dropped one of us already. What's to stop you from killing us too?"

"I am not like you. I do not shoot unarmed men."

"On your word, then," Morton said and threw his gun down. He nodded at Baker to do likewise. "It's our only chance."

Baker gave a small shake of his head, but let his gun fall to the ground. "I don't like it none."

Billy slowly slid his revolver into its holster. "Follow William back to the cabin. I'll ride drag, make sure no one gets lost."

William looked around in confusion. Chagrined, he realized he didn't know the way to the river. "Maybe you should lead," he said to Billy.

Billy shook his head and gave William a wry smile. "One of you Coe brothers, lead us back."

William rode close behind the unarmed Morton and Baker as Frank Coe led them to the cabin. "Where is Jesse?" William asked as they picked their way through the brown tufts of grass that poked up through the residual snow.

"He cut out a while ago," Morton said. "He could be anywhere by now."

"You were waiting at his c-c-cabin. Was he supposed to meet you there?"

Morton twisted around in his saddle to smirk at William.

William shrugged, though the motion was exaggerated by a spasm of his shoulder. "I would be worried if I were you," he said to Morton. "Who do you think will be the first to die in a g-g-gunfight?" He pointed at Morton's empty holster. "You are not exactly dressed for the occasion, and Billy is m-m-madder than a kicked rattler."

Morton turned back to look sullenly at the ground. "You promised us safe passage back to Lincoln."

"Not if there is a g-g-gunfight."

"Look, it's Jesse's cabin, and if he turns up there sooner or later, it's no doing of ours," Baker said. "Just get us back to Lincoln."

William ignored his plea. "How many men does Jesse have with him?"

Baker shrugged. "I don't know. Sometimes five or six, sometimes just one or two."

William gazed into the distance, felt warmth in the wind as it blew from the west. "Must be only one or two this t-t-time," he told Baker. "If it were more, you would be willing to take your chances and offer to lead us to them instead of g-g-going back to Lincoln."

"Shut up," Morton hissed at Baker.

When they got closer to the river, William recognized the woodsy defile wherein lay Jesse's cabin hideout. Billy bade them halt and he went into the cabin. He reemerged a few minutes later.

"Cabin's empty. We'll go back to our camp and wait it out there." He motioned to the three unsaddled horses still tied up in front. "Take those mounts back with us."

As the Coe brothers rounded them up, William turned to Billy. "Besides Morton and Baker, there was a third man in the cabin. Hoot. I shot him as they made their escape out the back door."

Billy nodded. "Let's go check."

A murder of scavenging crows marked the spot where a body lay. Billy prodded it with his boot. "Joe Turner. One of Dolan's men."

"One of the ones who killed John?"

"No, but a Dolan man just the same." Billy looked thoughtful for a moment. "Hadn't seen him around since the killing. I think he was sent on ahead to provision this cabin; Jesse, or Dolan, was preparing a hidey-hole if things got real bad in town." Billy smiled and winked. "I'll drape his body over one of those spare horses, and we'll take it back to town. I'll enjoy dumping this scum on the front porch of the House."

As Billy and the Coe brothers prepared to leave, William investigated the lean-to. He found hay bedding for horses, some oats stored in a bin, and a saddle with a broken strap. He took a handful of the oats to Sunfish.

Finished with the cabin, the party mounted and headed back toward their camp in the glade. William concentrated on his surroundings, laying a mental path back to it so that when they reached the grove of trees, he had a good idea how to find the cabin again.

William followed their prisoners into the sheltered spot and saw that Brewer and McNab had come with the supplies. McCloskey had climbed down from his perch on the rock and was building a campfire while Brewer talked to him.

Billy scowled at the campfire and then motioned for their two captives to dismount and sit with their backs to the rock wall. He bound their hands with a short rope. "Guess we'll stay the night," Billy said. He frowned at McCloskey. "Bank that fire so it doesn't smoke so much."

William unsaddled Sunfish and set his tack near to Billy's. "We could make it b-b-back to Lincoln today. Any p-p-particular reason you want to stay the night?"

"I've been thinking about something, and I want to work it out before we get back to town."

"What is it? Do you think Jesse will try to r-r-rescue Morton and Baker?"

"I wish we would be that lucky." Billy looked up at the darkening sky stretched out over them like black canvas.

"I'm gonna make a play when it gets full dark. Will you back me?"

William's tongue began to tingle, and he hesitated. Some evil was brewing, but he couldn't put his finger on it. On the other hand, he didn't want Billy to think that he was unreliable.

"Sure. What d-d-do you have in mind?"

Billy sucked in a breath over clenched teeth. "I'm just gonna simplify things."

Trial at Twilight

H ot beans and hard bread made up the supper that night. William sat on his haunches in the shadow of the rock and out of the firelight.

How did Billy mean to simplify things? Jesse's cabin was less than a mile away. Perhaps Billy insisted on staying the night just to draw Jesse out, hoping that with William's help the scores could be settled in a single gunfight.

William hunkered down between the prisoners and the tethered horses. The glade grew darker, and stars struggled to life in the sky. A creeping tension tightened William's shoulders. He listened for the soft, out-of-place sound. The snap of twig. A brush of leaf when the wind stilled.

Billy clanged his tin plate as he scraped the leavings and interrupted William's thoughts. It seemed a signal of some sort, for conversation around the fire ceased.

Drawing his revolver, Billy slowly turned the cylinder and inspected the chambers one by one. *Click . . . click . . . click.* "McCloskey, untie the prisoners."

McCloskey pulled a knife from his boot and swiftly cut their bonds. "What's going on, Billy?" he asked when they were free.

Billy looked at Baker and Morton. "I'm having second thoughts about taking you two to Lincoln."

Morton stared at him like a mesmerized rat at a rattler. "Why?"

"It means a trial and really we don't need one. I saw you murder Mr. Tunstall. And while the lawyers confusticate everything, Brady's friends will let you slip jail just like Brady let you slip town yesterday."

"Brady didn't let us slip town yesterday," Baker said. "We weren't wanted for anything and had a right to go where we wished."

Billy shook his head, his eyes taking on that nutty look again. He waved his gun at Baker. "And where you wished to go was to leave town in the middle of a snowstorm? No, you were running, running from me. Brady told you we had warrants for you. He said as much when we arrested him."

"Not true," Morton spluttered.

Billy turned the gun on him. "See, this is why a trial is unnecessary. You just lie." He took a breath. "William, when we told Brady we had warrants for Morton and Baker, what did he say?"

"That he did not care if we had chicken s-s-scrawls from a federal marshal."

"Exactly. Now what would make him say that if he didn't know we had warrants? What Brady did was to tell you two to get out of town until he could handle things."

"What are you going to do, Billy?" Baker said, eyes wide and reflecting the dancing flames of the campfire.

"Find you guilty, and kill you."

"I'm unarmed," Morton said.

Billy drew a second revolver from beneath his drover's coat. "So was Mr. Tunstall. Only we'll do it differently this time. I am going to give you this gun *before* I shoot you." He flipped it to land at Morton's feet.

McCloskey moved to stand between Billy and the prisoners. "Don't do this, Billy. This is murder. We have the law on our side now. Don't make us outlaws."

"What do you say, William?" Billy asked.

What could he say? Billy's intent to murder the prisoners shocked William, but his promise to back the kid held him in place for the first few moments. He agreed with Billy; these men should die. But like this? Many men had fallen to William, but none in cold-blooded murder.

"I do not shoot unarmed men. But if you give them a gun . . ."

"Is it even loaded?" McCloskey asked, scooping the gun from the ground.

"I don't want it," Morton said.

"Get out of the way, McCloskey," Billy said.

"No, Billy," McCloskey said. "I won't let you do this."

Billy relaxed and made as if to return his gun to his holster. "That's what I figured. You have been in with them all along. I just had to prove it. Simplifies things this way." He stepped to the side.

"What are you talking about? I was just stopping you from committing murder." McCloskey's shoulders slumped as he relaxed.

His hand a blur, Billy fired past McCloskey into Morton's chest.

McCloskey's eyes widened and his mouth dropped open.

Baker turned, pale-faced, to William. "You prom—"

Billy shot Baker in the head.

"Hoot," William said, shocked. "Hoot, hoot."

"Billy!" McCloskey shouted, making a move to grab at Billy's gun hand. He stopped with his arm half raised, for Billy swung his gun to aim at the center of McCloskey's chest.

Murder reflected in Billy's crazed eyes.

Friends No More

"You are a traitor, McCloskey." Billy's voice was steely and his hand steady.

"No, I only wanted to see them get a fair trial—"

Billy cut him off. "Yesterday, you warned Morton and Baker we were coming for them. You went to Wortley's for breakfast, but first you stopped by the House. And then you stalled for time until you saw us coming up the street."

"I did no such thing." McCloskey rubbed a palm over a sweating brow. "I'm a Regulator, same as you."

"Maybe you was at first, right after Mr. Tunstall was kilt. That made you mad. But your old ties with Baker got in the way and ya warned him."

McCloskey looked around at the other men, eyes fox-wary as the hounds closed in. "I say that I didn't. This time you didn't witness what you claim, and I demand to be taken back to Lincoln to explain things."

"No need," Billy said, cocking his revolver. "Brady as much as pointed his finger at you."

"I was there when you arrested him, and he did no such thing." McCloskey splayed his fingers, palms out toward Billy.

"Sure he did. He said he didn't care if we had *federal* warrants. No one knew about the warrants but us Regulators, and we had just gotten into town the night before with them. One of us told Brady. It was you."

McCloskey splayed his fingers, palms out toward Billy. "Wait, Billy, wait—"

Billy's Colt Thunderer roared. The bullet passed between McCloskey's outstretched hands and hammered him dead center.

McCloskey's eyes went wide, and his hands clutched at the hole in his chest. A great sadness fell over his features, and he collapsed to the ground.

Billy holstered his still smoking six-gun. "Anyone object?"

"That wasn't right, Billy." Brewer grasped Billy's shoulder. "He was one of us; we should have taken him in and let him explain it."

"He was a traitor. Traitors get no quarter from me." Billy shrugged off Brewer's hand and turned to William. "Well, this makes three of mine to your five."

William's hands shook. The impact of the murder left his head twirling a Virginia reel. He couldn't wrap his thoughts around the fact that his friend was actually counting the slain. He staggered, arms flailing for balance. "Swinging, dinging. Mine were in gunfights, yours were unarmed."

"Dead is dead. And not an innocent among them."

William looked around at Brewer and the Coe brothers. "What about you? Hoooot! Do you go along with this?"

Brewer shook his head. "You heard me tell Billy it was wrong. We should've taken McCloskey back to Lincoln, given him a chance to explain hisself."

"Yes, I heard you. But that is not the question now. The question is what are you g-g-going to do about McCloskey's murder?"

"What can we do?" Frank Coe asked. "As Billy said, dead is dead. A shame, but it's done now."

"C'mon," George Coe said. "We're Regulators. We have the power to enforce the law, and if that means cleaning the traitors from our ranks, I'm all for it. I mean, it's not like McCloskey was innocent." He turned to Billy. "You shoulda been a lawyer, kid."

"So the question is what are you gonna do about it, Hoots?" Billy asked.

"Do not call me that. Only my friends may call me Hoots."

"You mean we ain't friends anymore?" Billy's eyes lost that nutty look and shone now with a watery film. He rubbed the heel of his hand across the bridge of his nose.

"This is not some prank among friends."

"I know." Billy sniffed, looking at the ground. Then his eyes sought William's and his voice firmed up. "Killing a man is serious business. But it is the business you're in."

William shook his head. "One week ago I had three good friends. Mr. Tunstall, Emily, and you. Fitting in with regular folk has meant everything to me. To lose that is to lose the only happiness in my life. But Tunstall is dead. Emily fled. And now you have mortally wounded the one friendship I had left."

"Remember who killed Tunstall." Billy huffed, gathering the Coe brothers and Brewer in with a glance. "Morton and Baker. They're the ones who drove Emily away. Why this fuss? They're dead, so good riddance."

William rubbed his brow. "I have killed many men. But never murder. It was always them or me. I got no pleasure out of killing them, except the uncertain joy of remaining alive."

Billy shrugged.

"You asked me to back you up," William said, "even though you knew you were going to m-m-murder three men. And you enjoyed it. If I am okay with this, then I am as good as a murderer myself."

"You make too much of this," Billy said. "We are in a war, and in case you haven't noticed, we are losing. The only one left of any consequence on our side is Alex McSween. We must protect him like the king in chess." He gestured at the three bodies. "This was just clearing the board of a knight and a few pawns."

"I am not a pawn to be used to further your own vengeance. Had you been straight with me, I might be able to still call you a friend. But I must live straight with myself."

"Whatever you say, Hoots." Billy turned away.

The name rankled—the final signal the cherished camaraderie with Billy was gone.

"You have made yourself an outlaw. I cannot r-r-ride with you." William picked up his saddle and tack and carried it to Sunfish. He scowled at Brewer and the Coe brothers. "None of you. The Regulators have become a band of murderers."

Frank Coe stared at him. "I'll be switched if I let some clown of a gunslinger lecture me."

Billy raised a hand to silence Frank and frowned at William. "Where're you goin'?"

"Back to Jesse's hideout. I have unfinished b-b-business with him."

"Don't be a fool. You're goin' alone. Jesse could show up with twenty men, and the rest of us are returning to Lincoln tomorrow."

William reached for the cinch straps under Sunfish's belly. "We may meet again. I will not t-t-turn my hand against you, but from now on, I r-r-ride alone."

Wilderness Again

Outside the shelter of the grove, the wind sawed through William's coat like wicked icy knives. William's anger kept him warm for the first few hundred yards. By then, the flickering campfire behind him had been swallowed by the dark night. His certainty he had to separate from Billy seemed less immediate now.

Though he had carefully marked a visual trail earlier that afternoon, he couldn't make out any of his landmarks. Maybe he should turn back. Billy would rib him for sure, but that isn't what stopped him. After all, William knew he could take a joke.

He settled back in his saddle and let Sunfish continue to pick his way through the rocks and scrub. Billy had been a friend who'd betrayed him. The pain of that, of friendship given and cruelly misused, made return impossible. To go back now would follow a trail with Billy that William could never ride.

The cold numbed his anger, as well as his nose and fingertips. Earlier fears of being lost in the wilderness surfaced. The first rat bites of anxiety nibbled at him.

William sat straighter in the saddle. He twisted his torso to peer around. Where would he go? A deeper darkness loomed to his right. He urged Sunfish toward it. A line of trees coalesced. Just riding between their trunks cut the wind, and William felt a little warmer.

He dismounted and tied Sunfish's reins to a low-hanging bough; the motion cascaded a thump of snow onto his shoulders. He scraped ineffectually at the frozen ground with his boot heel. Ice cover soddened fallen branches.

Terror of freezing icicled into his mind. This fear brought no dark tornado, reminding him nature did not present a target to a gunman, no matter how fast his draw. Against nature, a solitary man had no chance; it took men banding together to survive.

Alone for the last three years, he had lived a solitary life. One man among anonymous others, until he met Emily. From their first blossoming friendship, other cherished relationships sprouted. Her brother. The McSweens. Billy. The Tunstall ranch hands. His loneliness spread out over a dozen or so other souls, bringing a welcome change from solitude.

Then one by one, violence tore the sweet bonds away. When he stormed away from Billy, it put paid to his obligations to all the Tunstall hands, cleared all debts to the other Regulators. Weariness filled him. He longed to lie down and sleep.

Sunfish roused him with a nose-butt and an insistent nickering.

William had one trusted friend left. He grasped Sunfish's loose reins. With a groaning effort, he pulled himself into the saddle and slumped over the horse's neck. Sunfish moved beneath him. Without further thought, he clung to the animal's mane.

Sunfish roused him again with a touch of his nose to William's boot.

William opened his eyes. A cabin stood a few feet away. Even in the dark he recognized it. Jesse's hideout, where earlier that day they had caught up with Baker and Morton.

He dismounted and, ignoring the lean-to in the back, led Sunfish through the cabin door. A few embers still smoldered in the fireplace. He added fuel from the wood stacked by the wall and fanned a blaze. Warmth returned.

With stiff fingers, he unsaddled Sunfish and threw the tack on the floor.

Covering himself with the saddle blanket, William stretched out by the fire with his unbuckled gun belts close to hand. The wind keened outside. He remembered an earlier night, his second night in Lincoln. He, Emily, and John had dined at Wortley's. The wind blew chill between the tables, isolating the little oil-burning heaters attempting to stave off the cold. John had called the cold blasts a lonely wind.

Except for his horse, William was alone. He succumbed to a deep weariness and slept.

THE END

About the Author

Robin Elno is a retired army colonel, semiretired psychiatrist, and full-time author. He lives in San Antonio, Texas, and is an active member of the San Antonio Writers' Guild. Inspired by famed neurologist Oliver Sacks and his work with neurological conditions like Tourette Syndrome, the author has created a unique and compelling character set against the backdrop of true, historical events.

IngramElliott
uncommon publishing

We delight in publishing the non-traditional, uncon-
ventional and alternative including:

Fiction
Metaphysical
Professional and Nonfiction
Romance
Young Adult
IE Snaps!

Review our list of themes and topics and perhaps they
will inspire you to consider writing for original genres
and audiences.

www.ingramelliott.com